SUPER #3
GOOFBALLS

Super Underwear...
and Beyond!

SUPER GOOFBALLS

Book One: That Stinking Feeling

Book Two: Goofballs in Paradise

SUPER #3
GOOFBALLS
Super Underwear...
and Beyond!

written and illustrated by
peter Hannan

HarperTrophy®
An Imprint of HarperCollinsPublishers

This book is dedicated to Ruby, the best daughter in this
or any other universe, real or imagined, now known or
hereafter created, without limitation, in perpetuity, amen.

Harper Trophy® is a registered trademark of
HarperCollins Publishers.

Super Goofballs, Book #3: Super Underwear . . . and Beyond!
Copyright © 2007 by Peter Hannan

Library of Congress Cataloging-in-Publication Data is available.
ISBN-10: 0-06-085215-1—ISBN-13: 978-0-06-085215-3

Typography by Joel Tippie
❖
First Harper Trophy edition, 2007

TABLE OF CONTENTS

CHAPTER 1

Mighty Terrible Situation

Mighty Tighty Whitey was one freaked-out pair of jockey shorts.

"Don't worry, Mum and Dad!" he shouted in his thick English accent, striking a super-heroic pose. *"I'm comin'!"*

Mayor What's-His-Name had just phoned to tell us that Lousy Lou the LaundroManiac had clothesnapped Jumpin' Jack Jockstrap and the Battlin' Bra of Birmingham, Mighty's super-hero parents.

Mighty was mighty upset. He tensed up and his elastic waist/head-band snapped shut. His face got

bright red and hot air built up inside. The air had to go somewhere, and it pushed up and out, causing the elastic to vibrate, making a super-high-pitched farting sound.

Blunder Mutt laughed so hard he fell on his face. He kept laughing as he stood up, dusted himself off, and fell on his face again.

Mighty Tighty Whitey was not amused. "I don't know what you find so bloomin' funny 'bout a supah bra and jockstrap gettin' clothesnapped!"

He whacked a nail into the floor with three superfast hammer whacks. Then he stretched the backside of his waist/headband up over the front side, hooked it on the nail, dug in his heels and leaned back, stretching all the way across the room.

"Jeepers-freepers, I wishes I could be makin' myself longer an' longer all aways crosstah room!" said Blunder Mutt.

"I think our friend Blunder means to say he wishes he were *stretchy*," I said.

"No," Blunder replied, a little annoyed, "Blunder meanded to say jeepers-freepers, I wishes I could be makin' myself longer an' longer all aways crosstah room!"

"All right, all right . . . stand back!" shouted Mighty Tighty Whitey, straining hard against the super tension of his elastic. "Fantastic! Elastic! Sarcastic!"

But just as Mighty Tighty Whitey was about to let go and fly through the window, the nail ripped a gaping hole through the fabric of his forehead—if a pair of underwear actually *has* a forehead—and he flew backwards instead,

into the kitchen-lair, and landed
with a crash into the open dishwasher/3D electron
probe analytic refractor. The impact
caused the door to slam shut and the
machine to turn on. We heard a muf-
fled "Blubba flah-bubbahboobly-
floobly!" from inside.

The Goofballs went
into superpanic mode.

And that's a lot of panicked goofballs: Blunder Mutt (the dumbest, bravest super lunatic ever), Super Vacation Man (vacation-obsessed avenger and Blunder's partner), Scoodlyboot (SVM's childhood dog, recently made young and beautiful again, and for some strange reason deeply in love with Blunder Mutt), Wonder Boulder (624 pounds of gung-ho super granite), Pooky the Paranormal Parakeet (tiny turban-wearing, mind-reading bird), SuperSass CuteGirl (supersassy, supercute, super girlish), the Impossibly Tough Two-Headed Infant (Biff and Smiff, super-musclebound, constantly arguing twins), the Frankenstein Punster (monstrous master of the bad joke), and T-Tex3000 (supersmall space-cowboy-dinosaur-headcase). Plus, the original residents: Granny (the Bodacious Backwards Woman) and me (Amazing Techno Dude). It was getting to be a super-full house.

We struggled to open the door, but Mighty was holding it closed from inside.

"Blubba flah-bubbah-boobly-floobly!" he yelled again.

"What the—*Splash! Sploosh! Splutter!*—is he trying to say?" said Super Vacation Man.

"MIGHTY'S SOAPING TO SAY SOMETHING, BUT HE IN BAD BUBBLE AND ALL WASHED UP," said the Punster.

"Are you about finished?" I said.

But Blunder Mutt understood Mighty. "Doze underprants speakish my languish!"

Turns out when you speak with a mouthful of soapy water, you're pretty much speaking Blunder Mutt's language.

"He saying dat if he can't even fly out a window—dah easierest ting *ever* fer underprants—then somebudda else better save his underprants parents, 'cause *dis* underprants is just not *super* nuff!"

"Can't do it?" I said. "He's usually such a confident guy. The most confident pair of underpants *I've* ever met."

I yanked with all my might on the dishwasher/refractor door and it flew open, letting out a huge cloud of steam. There was Mighty Tighty Whitey

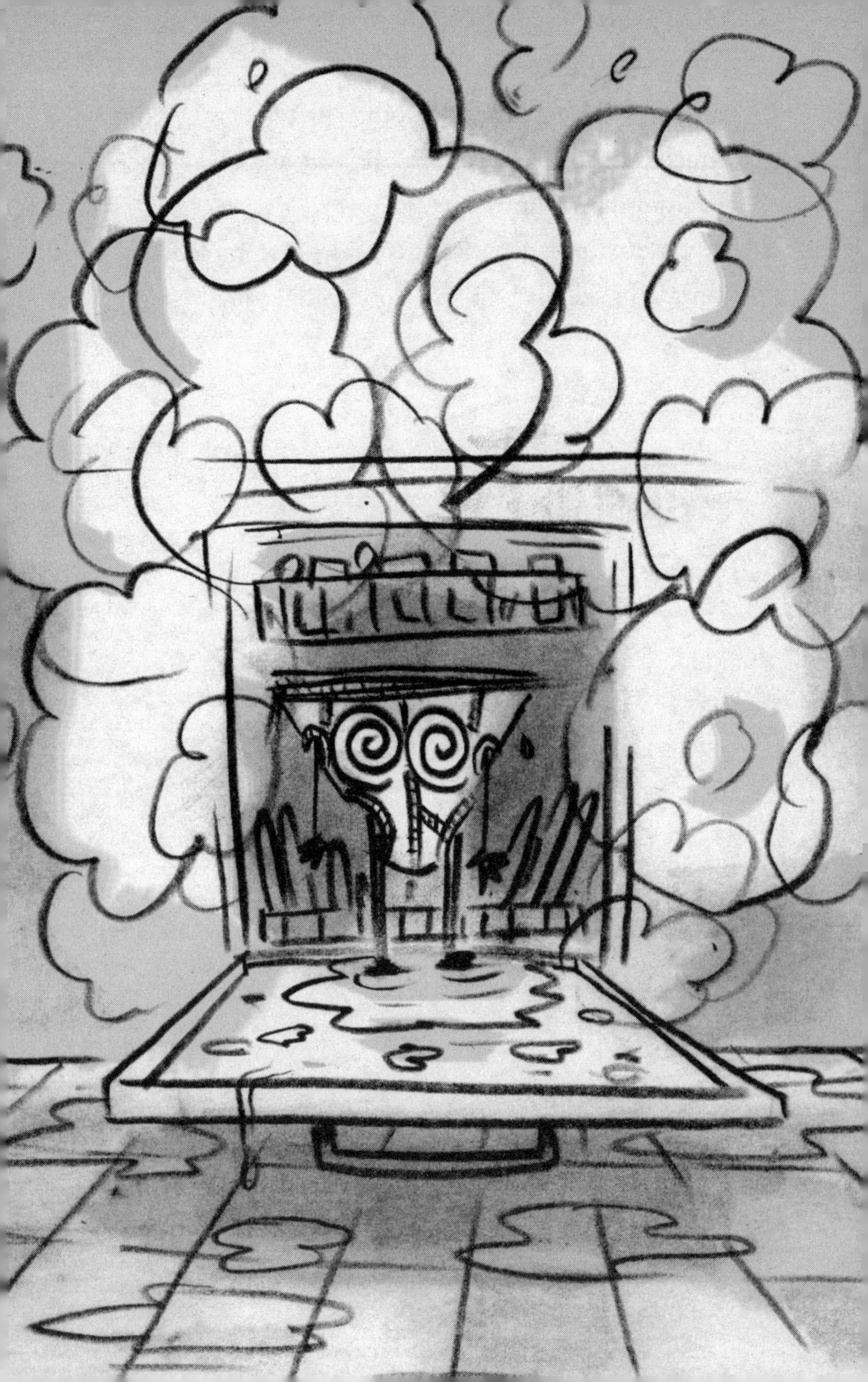

standing among the dripping plates, cups, and refracted things. He was soaking wet and all spaced-out from the steamy heat.

His eyes rolled backwards and he stumbled forwards. He fell flat on the floor with a loud, soggy *thwack*.

CHAPTER 2

unsure underpants

I revived him with a bucket of cold water.

"Me mum and dad were right," he blubbered. "I ain't supah enough."

He told us that he had left home because his parents babied him too much. They felt he was too young to be a superhero. They insisted on calling him "Itty Bitty Pants."

I knew how he felt. Granny (the Bodacious Backwards Woman) used to treat me like that, too. Even though she now knew I was a superhero myself, she still babied me sometimes. "Cold it's! Up bundle!" and, of course the old standby, "Asparagus your eat!"

Mighty and his parents had a terrible argument when he left. "Who needs family?" he said as he walked away. "I'm an important pair of super underpants now!" But he was just talking tough. He loved his mom and dad and missed them a lot. Now he wanted to rescue them, but he was worried that they had been right all along.

"C'mon, Mighty!" I said. "Pick yourself up and wring yourself out! Tell you what. I'll come with you. We'll work together on this case, and if it works out, you can be my permanent sidekick. I don't know a darn thing about the seamy underworld of super undergarments, so you *have* to do it! You're the only one who *can* do it!"

Mighty struggled to his feet. He was still droopy from all of the water. "Yeah, *right*," he said sarcastically. "I can do it."

"This is no time for sarcasm!" I said. "You really *can* do it."

"You seriously think I can do it?" He smiled.

And then all the Super Goofballs yelled, *"Yes!"* with such enthusiasm that the wind from that shout knocked Mighty Tighty Whitey over again, flat on his back.

Everyone helped him up. Biff and Smiff wrung the water out of him, SuperSass CuteGirl dried him with a hair dryer, and Granny sewed up his rip with a few superfast backwards stitches. Pretty soon he was almost looking like a super pair of underpants again.

CHAPTER 3
underwear 101

"**B**y the way, Mighty," I said, "I've been meaning to ask you: What's the deal with you and your parents? I mean, not all underwear is super, or even *alive*, for that matter."

"Okay," said Mighty, "I'll give you a crash course in Underpantology. Correct. Most underwear is not alive. Like the kind of underwear you're all wearing now."

"Not me," said Wonder Boulder.

"Nor me," said Pooky. "I wear under*feathers*, not under*wear*."

"Under where?" said Blunder Mutt.

"Okay, stop," said Mighty. "Like *most* of you are wearing. Lemme ask you somethin', Goofballs. Any of you ever lost a sock?"

"Not me," said Wonder Boulder.

"I've lost lots of socks," I said.

"And I suppose you've lost underwear?"

"Of course," I said.

"No, you haven't."

"Yes, I have."

"You didn't *lose* them, they *ran away*."

"That's the craziest thing I've ever heard," I said.

"Dat's da troof. Mine never runned away and me have da same underwear under dere my whole life," said Blunder Mutt.

"Like, did we *really* need to know that?" said SuperSass.

"Well, Blundah, some underwear's got it, and some ain't," said Mighty. "I come from a part o' town called the Lost Undergarment District. It's a bloomin' parallel world where runaway undergarments of all kinds—doctors, lawyers, students, teachahs, and mums and dads—live, work, and play. Me mum and dad 'appen ta be undergarment supahheroes. And now they've been clothesnapped."

CHAPTER 4
LET IT BE ME

Of course, all the Super Goofballs wanted to come along. "Me!" "Me!" "Me!" "Me!" "Me!" "Oh, why don't the rest of you, like, just grow up?" said SuperSass. "Okay, where was I? Oh, yeah: ME!"

The Impossibly Tough Two-Headed Infant claimed that he/they should get to go because he/they are diaper experts, and diapers are just like underwear. "Only more comfy!" shouted Biff. "And more convenient!" said Smiff.

I had my doubts, but

Granny said, "Idea fine a like sounds!" and Mighty Tighty Whitey and I didn't feel like arguing.

"Okay, but no more!" I insisted.

"'Cept me," said Blunder Mutt, "'cause I da bestest a da bunchest and I want to meet an underwears doctor because I is a doctor of answer-da-phone-ology."

Scoodlyboot, the prettiest dog on the planet, blew air kisses at him.

"Stop that you not-at-all-pretty dog I gots no interesht in kissin'!" growled Blunder. And then, back to his superhappy self, he jumped up and down and shouted, "But *yes*, I is comin' and Supers Vacationy Man comin', too, 'cause I kicks his sides for him! *Yes! Yes! Yessy yes!*"

"No, Blunder," I replied. "You and Super Vacation Man are staying here."

SVM didn't want to come anyway. He had just settled into the wading pool.

But my words hit Blunder hard and he hit the floor even harder. Then he sat up and stayed like a good dog, but pouted like a spoiled kid. All the Super Goofballs were pouting.

"I'm sorry," I said, "but I can only handle so many goofballs at one time!"

Then Mighty Tighty Whitey, the Impossibly Tough Two-Headed Infant, and I headed out the door and down Thirteenth Street. Our mission: to rescue Jumpin' Jack Jockstrap and the Battlin' Bra of Birmingham from the dastardly clutches of Lousy Lou the LaundroManiac.

CHAPTER 5
Home un-improvement

Mighty's neighborhood was like a different world. A washed-out dingy gray world. The only sound was a whispery wind that whistled through the empty streets. With that wind came the unmistakable smell of underwear.

Mighty's childhood home was an apartment building that looked a lot like a clothes dresser. As we climbed the drawer-steps up to Mighty's place, it became clear that every drawer-apartment in the building was empty. Whoever lived there had moved out in a hurry. When we got to the top floor, we squeezed into Mighty's family's cramped underwear drawer-apartment to look for clues.

It looked like the place had been hit by a tornado. Every piece of furniture was broken to bits. The

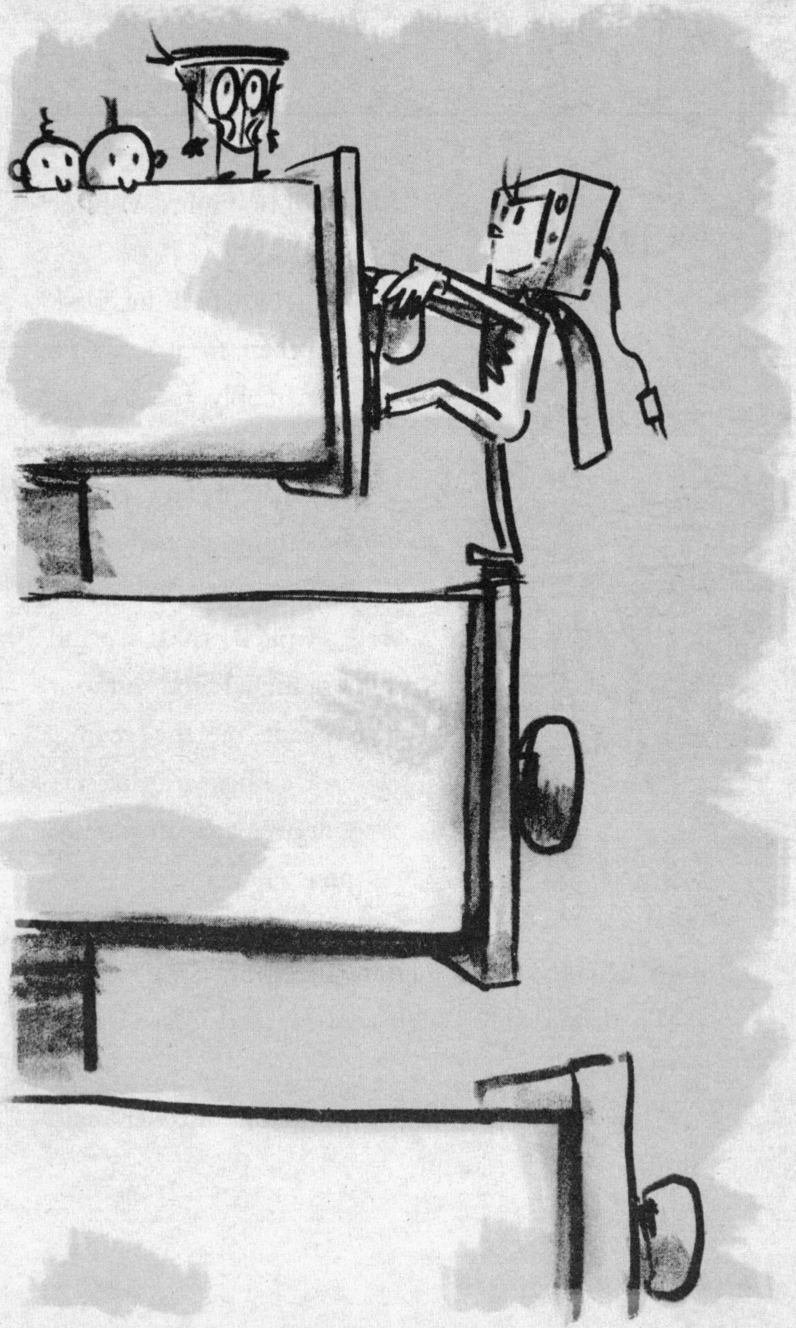

apartment was full of soap-suds: lots of dirty, scummy soapsuds.

Mighty Tighty Whitey was in shock.

"Why, why, why?!" he cried.

Just then, from behind a pile of bubbly rubble that looked like it might once have been a couch, something popped out.

It startled us so much that we all jumped and hit our heads on the ceiling. Ceilings in dresser-drawer-apartments are pretty low.

"Woy? I'll tell ye woy, boyo!" shouted that something in a strong Irish brogue.

The Impossibly Tough Two-Headed Infant leaped at the thing.

"Take *that*," said Biff. "You stinking intruder!" said Smiff.

But the thing simply stepped aside and the twins crashed into a wall.

Crash.

"Ouch," said Biff.

"Me, too," said Smiff.

And to the floor. *Thud.*

"Ouch again."

"Me, too, again. Stinking intruder."

Mighty Tighty Whitey raised an eyebrow. "Technically, he's not an intrudah, but he certainly does stink."

"I shant be believin' that a spic-and-span someone such as meself could possibly be stinkin' as much as a wee pair o' Itty Bitty Pants," said the thing, which looked like a sock. A *lot* like a sock. He *was* a sock.

"I told you *never* ta call me that, you blabber-mouthing bloke!" Mighty Tighty Whitey leaped at the sock as if he was going to slug him in the mouth, which was located in the *toe* part of his sock head.

They leaned in close to each other, sneering and shaking their fists.

"Let me guess," I said. "You two know each other."

"Right," said Mighty. "Meet my Irish cousin, Terrifyin' Tubesock Lad."

"We're *related*," said the tubesock, "but we can't *relate* ta each other, if ya catch me drift."

"Well," I said, "what on earth are you doing here, hiding behind the couch and jumping out and scaring us like that?"

"I have ta live up ta me name, now don't I?" he said. "Plus, I've been lookin' fer clues just like you. And I 'appen ta know a ting 'r two about what 'appened ta his ma 'n' da!"

"Could you kindly speak *English*, you blarney-barking potato muncher?" said Mighty

Tighty Whitey. "What in the world is a *ma 'n' da*?"

"I'm spakin' about me poor, sweet aunt 'n' uncle what unfortunately brought you *inta* th' world!"

Both of them were pretty hard to understand.

"Mighty," I said, "I think the sock is talking about your mum and dad."

"Right you are," said Tubesock. "And the very reason they got themselves snatched up in the first place is due ta the fact that they were out lookin' fer their ungrateful wee sonny boy!"

CHAPTER 6
The Tubesock Talks

Tubesock filled us in. LaundroManiac ran a money laundering and counterfeiting ring and was snatching all the socks and underwear of the Lost Undergarment District, because, as everyone knows, money is made of paper with fabric in it.

"So," said Terrifyin' Tubesock Lad, "all these poor undergarments will be washed, rinsed, dried, shredded, mixed with paper 'n' made inta pulp, flattened, printed, 'n' chopped up inta dollar bills! And that, my so-called mighty cousin, includes yer dear ol' ma 'n' da!"

Now Mighty Tighty Whitey was even more alarmed. He held a finger up in the air and shouted, "Fantastic, Elastic, Sarcastic . . . Mum and Dad, 'ere I come!" He lifted a foot, as if he was going to take a huge step forward, but then stopped, balancing on the other foot. "Where are we going?"

"Good question," said Terrifyin' Tubesock Lad. "Let's 'ave a think."

Then he leaned against the wall to have a think. But the wall was a swinging door and Tubesock fell right through it.

CHAPTER 7
Down in the Alley

It was a secret door in the house that he grew up in, but Mighty had never known it was there. His parents, like most superheroes, had secret exits in their houses. This one was like a laundry chute. We all followed Tubesock through and tumbled into the dark. We bounced, rolled, and slid down a steep slide, slamming into the sides of the passageway all the way down. Finally, we landed in a heap. I looked around and saw we were in the alley behind the apartment building.

We stood up and realized we were covered from head to toe with what looked like a mixture of dirt and laundry detergent. In fact, it *was* a mixture of dirt and laundry detergent. It was blowing and drifting through the alley like gray snow.

I saw something move out of the corner of my eye. It was a tiny something across the alley. It was hard to see because it was exactly the same dingy gray color as everything else. It was waving at us.

As we moved closer, we realized that it was a very tiny sock with a nametag that read "Billy Bob Sweetums." His huge, pale blue eyes seemed too big for his little face. And he was shaking with fear. He was trying to talk.

"Lawn . . ." he said in a tiny, terrified whisper. He said it again and again. "Lawn . . . Lawn . . . Lawn . . ."

He was obviously lost
and looking for his lawn.

"Where do you live,
Billy Bob?"

"Lawn . . ."

"Yes, well, your lawn
is probably behind your *house*, so where's your *house*?"

"Lawn . . ."

"Okay, where are your parents, Billy Bob?"

"Lawn . . ."

"Do you prefer *Sweetums*?"

"Lawn . . ."

This was getting kinda spooky.

And it got even spookier, because then more socks and undergarments started coming out from behind walls, baskets, and detergent dunes, all saying, "Lawn . . . lawn . . . lawn . . ." Sort of like the Munchkins in Munchkinland, but instead of little people, they were socks, boxer shorts, jockey shorts, stretched-out grandpa underwear, huge granny girdles—every kind of sock and undergarment, in every size and shape. Some were dirty, some clean, some wet, some dry.

"After all," said Mighty Tighty Whitey, "some escape on the way to the washer, some on the way to the *dryer*, and some just tunnel out through the back walls of underwear drawers."

"I noticed a hole in the back of *my* drawer," I said, "but I thought it was just mice."

"No," said Mighty, "it was *me*."

CHAPTER 8

LONG TIME NO SEE

Now that was a shocker. Mighty told me that he had started out as a pair of my underwear.

"I thought you looked familiar," I said.

But he ran away before I had even opened the plastic package he came in. He knew from the start that he was *that* kind of underwear.

"It was completely impossible to breathe in there," he said.

He made it all the way to the Lost Undergarment District on his own but then realized he had no place

to stay. And that's when Jumpin' Jack Jockstrap and the Battlin' Bra of Birmingham took

him in. They took in lots of
young runaway socks and
underwear. They knew how
hard life on the street could
be because they had been run-
aways themselves. They met in
a trunk on a steamship en route
from London and ran away
together and got married as soon as
they hit Gritty City. Mighty and his many
brothers and sisters were sewn in factories all
over the world, but they all spoke with the thick
English accent of their adopted mum and dad. They
lived together in the small Lost Undergarment
District apartment until one day, two books ago,
Mighty Tighty Whitey saw an ad in the back of the
Super Globe Gazette and knocked on our door at 1313
Thirteenth Street.

So this was a reunion for Mighty and me, even
though back when the Bodacious Backwards Woman
first bought him and put him in my drawer, we had
no idea that he was, you know, one of the *live* ones.

CHAPTER 9
panic in pantytown

Meanwhile, here in this back alley of the Lost Undergarment District, all the residents looked absolutely terrified.

"What are they so scared of?" I wondered.

"Scared they'll get scooped up," said Tubesock.

I reassured them. "You've got nothing to worry about."

Then I leaned in close to Billy Bob Sweetums. "Nobody's getting scooped up while *we're* on the job."

Just then, the street began to shake. It felt like an earthquake. Next there was a roaring, screeching of brakes, skidding of tires, and around the corner came the loudest truck I'd ever heard. Gray smoke poured out of its huge exhaust pipes, and the roaring and screeching got so loud it felt like a hundred hammers were hammering my head.

As scared as all those undergarments looked before, now they looked ten times as scared. Their eyes got gigantic and they finally found the word that they'd all been trying to say.

"*LaundroManiac!*" they screamed.

The undergarments turned to run for cover, but before they could take a step, large nets on the end of long poles extended from the sides of the truck and started scooping them up.

The first one to go was the little sock, and as he was being scooped he finally said something other than *lawn* or *LaundroManiac*. He screamed, "Nooooooooooooooooooooooooooooooooooooooooo ooooooooooooooooooooooooooooooooooooooooooooooo ooooooooooooooooooooooooooooooooooooooooooooo oooooooooooooooooooooooooooooooooooooooooooo ooooooooooooooooooooooooooooooo!"

This set a new world record for time passed during a single syllable.

The truck drove madly in circles until every undergarment had been scooped up and tossed into the back.

There was a sign on the side of the truck:

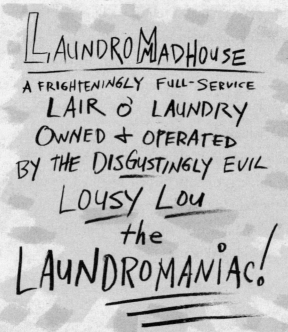

LaundroMadhouse
A FRIGHTENINGLY FULL-SERVICE
LAIR O' LAUNDRY
OWNED & OPERATED
BY THE DISGUSTINGLY EVIL
LOUSY LOU
the
LAUNDROMANIAC!

I got a good look at LaundroManiac through the windshield—at least his huge head. His face was bright white with a soapy, bluish tint. Even the pupils of his eyes were white—almost as white as the whites of his eyes. He was foaming at the mouth. He looked rabid, but the foam was actually soapsuds.

He drove off and yelled something that I couldn't understand. But as he yelled, he spewed soapsuds. Not clean bubbles, like in a bathtub; these were oily and dirty—more like bubbles in a polluted river. They ran down his chin and out the truck window like a washing machine runoff hose. It was disgusting. He also had what looked like the worst case of dandruff I've ever seen; it was actually powdered clothes-washing detergent. His hair was completely caked with the stuff and it flew from his head like snowflakes in the wind. He was disgustingly evil.

"Hey, Amazing Techno Dude," said Tubesock, "I t'ought ya said nobody was gettin' scooped up while we're on the job."

"I guess maybe . . ." said Biff.

" . . . we weren't technically on the job yet," said Smiff.

CHAPTER 10

FOLLOW THAT MANIAC!

Mighty Tighty Whitey quickly hammered one of his nails into the ground, hooked himself on it, and stretched back and back and back. We all jumped inside him and shot off in the direction of the speeding truck. We hit the back door with a thud and slid down to the bumper. The truck was going fast and it was hard to hold on. In fact, if it weren't for the superstrength of the Impossibly Tough Two-Headed Infant, we would have been super roadkill. They gripped the bumper

with their superstrong baby fingers. You know how babies have that instant finger-gripping reflex? Well, multiply that by . . . well, by a really big number. We hung on to their feet like a chain. Then we climbed up that chain one by one until we were all standing on the bumper, holding on for dear life, looking in through the rear window.

Mighty Tighty Whitey saw his parents inside. They were caught in a tangle of other undergarments inside an open laundry basket. They couldn't see us, but we could see that they were very upset. They were calling for help.

"Moity! Moity Toity! Moity Toity Woity!"

Their accents were thick.

The truck came to a screeching halt at the loading dock of a huge industrial building: The LaundroMadhouse.

"Looks like this could be the evil lair of LaundroManiac," said Mighty Tighty Whitey.

"Are you tinkin' that due ta the fact that there's a big sign, plain as day, sayin', 'Welcome ta the LaundroMadhouse, the Official Evil Lair of Lousy Lou the LaundroManiac'?" said the Terrifyin' Tubesock Lad.

"No, I'm thinkin' that due ta the fact that you should be wearin' a big sign, plain as day, sayin' 'Hi, My Name is Official Big Idiot'!" said Mighty Tighty Whitey.

While they bickered, LaundroManiac's Laundro-goons unloaded the truck. All the undergarments and socks were tossed into large laundry hampers on wheels, which were slowly winding like a train through the huge doors of the LaundroMadhouse, on their way to a conveyor belt that would take them through the washing, rinsing, drying, shredding, flattening, printing, and chopping rooms. Not good.

CHAPTER 11

GOON ENOUGH

The place was crawling with Laundrogoons. They looked a bit like Bigfoot, Bigfoots, Bigfeet, whatever—huge, sharp-toothed, furry monsters—except more disgusting. The fur looked like blue-gray lint from a clothes dryer. Mixed in with the lint was other stuff: human hair, used Band-Aids, toothpicks, dental floss, keys, coins, sticks, stones, small rodents, frogs—anything that might get stuck in the lint trap of a dryer. With all that stuff sticking out, they looked like gigantic, scary porcupines.

We had to figure out a way to get by them. This was easy enough for Mighty and Tubesock. They could just hop into one of the hampers—they'd fit right in. The twins just pulled their diaper up over their heads and looked like a plain old diaper—with legs. But I needed a disguise, so I quickly took off my underwear and pulled it over *my* head. This reminded me of a nightmare I'd had once. It was embarrassing, but when you're a superhero on a mission, there's no time for embarrassment. We hopped into a hamper.

We rode along with the rest of the undergarments— all whimpering and crying, terrified of what lay ahead. Peering over the top of our hamper, we kept our eyes open for Mighty's parents, for Billy Bob

Sweetums, and, of course, for LaundroManiac. The LaundroMadhouse was an amazingly huge building. It felt like a city inside. The roar of machinery—plus constant shredding, chopping, sloshing, and screaming—made it

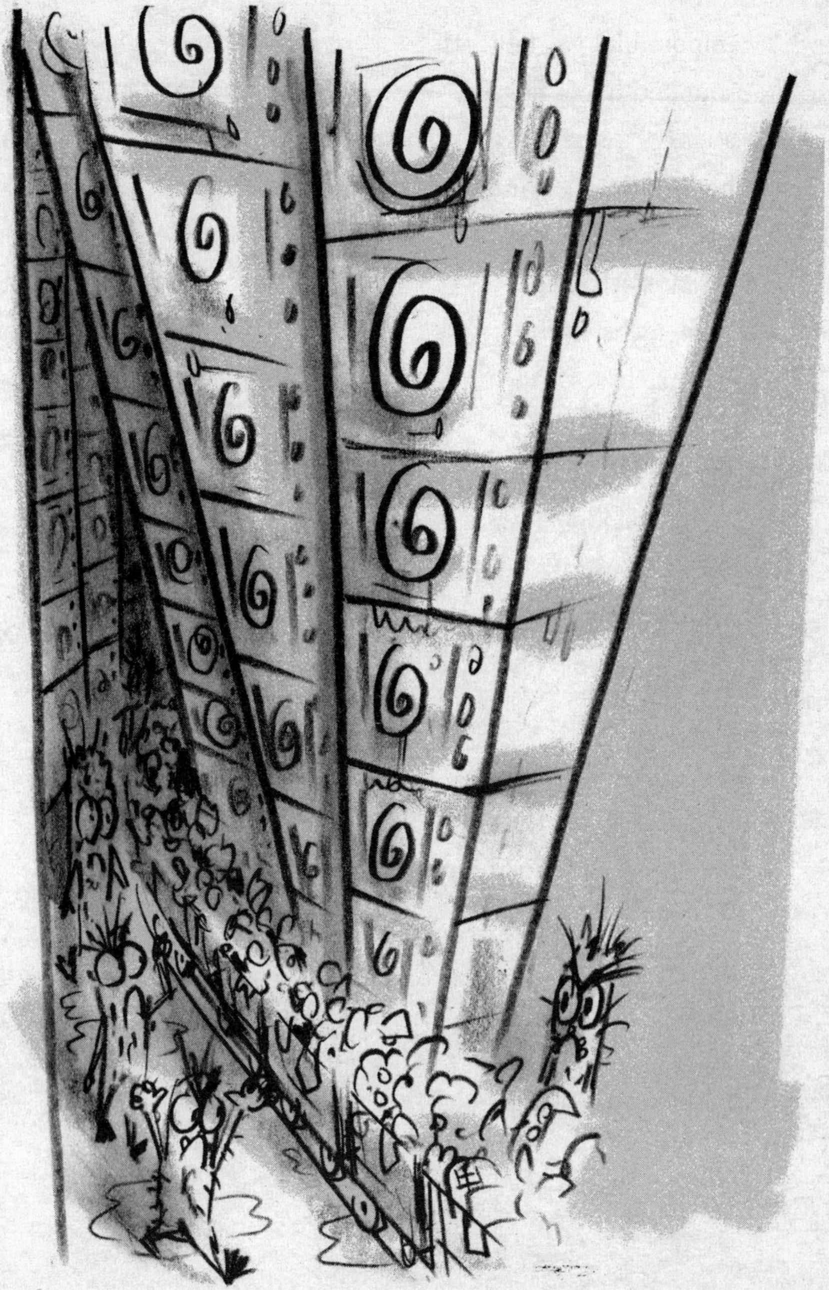

impossible to talk. It
sounded like a factory,
a laundry, and a mad-
house all rolled into
one. The walls were
lined with super
high-tech wash-
ing machines and
dryers that towered

like skyscrapers toward unbelievably high ceilings.

The whole time we rode along, Mighty Tighty
Whitey and Terrifyin' Tubesock Lad argued. Have
you ever known people who argue just for the sake
of argument? One says something and the other
immediately says the opposite?

"Good morning!"
"No, it's not!" "Yes,
it is!" "No!" "Yes!"
"No!" And pretty
soon, the stupid argu-
ment is a serious one?

"Of course, I'll be
the first ta see me parents," said
Mighty Tighty Whitey.

"Sorry, boyo—that'll be me," said Tubesock.

"They are *me* parents and I'll see 'em and save 'em,"

"You couldn't find yer underwear if you weren't yer underwear!"

"I can't believe I'm arguin' with a sock!"

"I can't believe I'm debatin' wit' a wee pair a Itty Bitty Pants!"

That was it—Mighty Tighty Whitey leaped at his cousin and their war of words turned into actual war.

They began wrestling and punching inside the hamper.

I really wanted to avoid being seen by the Laundrogoons and this wasn't going to help. "Can you two possibly cool it?" I said. But no.

Mighty snapped Tubesock repeatedly in the face with his super-elastic head/waistband.

Thwack! Thwack! Thwack! "I'll thwack ya back ta St. Paddy's Day!"

Tubesock started showing off his superpowers, too. Although most of his body was made of soft, knitted material—not exactly the most threatening substance—since his head contained his brain, and his incredible stubbornness made his brain as hard as a rock, his head was a deadly weapon. He whipped it

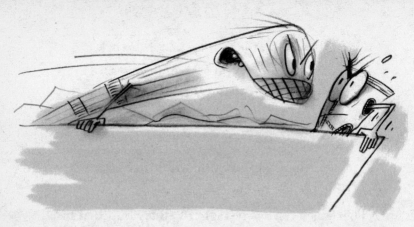

around in circles, stretching his sock body like a sling-shot and slamming his head into Mighty Tighty Whitey. The other undergarments in the hamper were getting knocked around pretty good, too. The hamper rocked back and forth wildly as we rolled along.

CHAPTER 12
Goon Crazy

O ne especially goony Laundrogoon noticed
what was going on and found it amusing that
a sock and a pair of underpants were fighting.

He spoke into a
walkie-talkie to
another goon.
"Eddie," he said,
"Freddie here.
Check out
the rockin'
sockin' under-
panties!"

I thought
that Mighty
and Tubesock

couldn't agree on anything, but they instantly agreed that this was an insult that could not go unanswered. They didn't stop fighting each other, though.

Bam! Bam! "Who might ya be spakin' of, ya big linty galoot?" called Tubesock.

Freddie the Laundrogoon got mad. "You couldn't possibly have *meant* to call me a big linty galoot!" he roared.

Thwack, thwack! "No," said Mighty Tighty Whitey. "What he *meant* ta call ya was a big linty *stupid* galoot!"

That did it. Freddie the Laundrogoon screamed into his walkie-talkie. "Backup! Backup! We've got a double disturbance in number forty-seven quadrant! Irish sock and English underpants in need of attitude adjustment! Send backup!"

An alarm went off and
a group of goons came
galloping out of a
control booth at
the very top of
a long metal
staircase.

They stampeded down the stairs, howling like . . . goons.

Tubesock jumped inside Mighty, and the twins and I pulled Mighty back and back and back, then let go, and Tubesock flew through the air like a missile. He slammed into the stomach of Freddie the Laundrogoon. Freddie fell over backwards, crashing into Eddie, who crashed into Neddie, who crashed into another goon whose name probably also rhymed, but which I didn't catch, and so on until they all went over like goony dominoes.

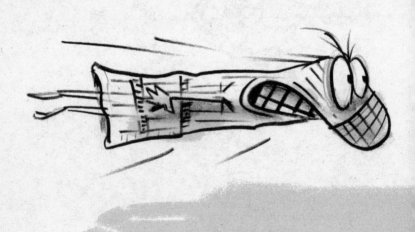

We jumped out of the hamper and sprinted up the stairs toward the control booth, which seemed to be the center of operations. It was a very, very, very long staircase. When we reached the top, we were out of breath and so far up we could barely hear the factory noise below. I peered in through the keyhole of the control booth door.

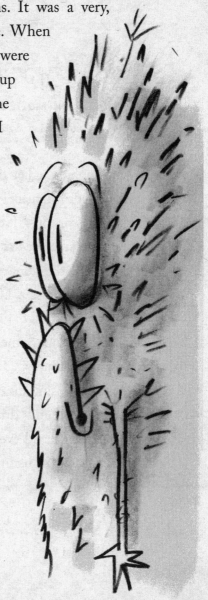

CHAPTER 13

MY MAIN MANIAC

Inside, looking uglier than ever, was Lousy Lou the LaundroManiac. He was surrounded by lots of Laundrogoons. I could see his huge head above theirs. He snickered to himself, looking through a long telescope at the laundry hampers below, winding their way toward disaster. He seemed to love gazing upon the vast viciousness of his moneymaking madness.

"I love gazing upon the vast viciousness of my moneymaking madness," he snickered through a clenched smile, causing disgusting bubbles to bubble through his teeth and dribble off his chin. The Laundrogoons snickered every time he snickered.

"Aren't I simply disgustingly evil?" he snickered.

"Yes, L.M., yes . . . *disgustingly* evil," snickered the Laundrogoons.

I was thinking about what our next move would be, trying to be as quiet as possible, but someone was making a lot of noise. When the Impossibly Tough Two-Headed Infant is out of breath, one twin breathes *in* loudly and the other breathes *out* loudly.

Biff was breathing in long, deep breaths that sounded like a very long-winded owl: "Whooooooo-ooooooooooooooooooooooooooooooooooooooooooooo..."

And Smiff was breathing out:

"Heeeeeeeeeeeeeeeeeeeeeeeeeeeeeeeeeeeeeeeeeeeee-
eeeeeeeeeeeeeeeeeeeee ..."

So, together:

"Whoooooooooooooooooooooooooooo ... heeee-
eeeeeeeeeeeeeeeeeeeeeeeeee ..."

Terrifyin' Tubesock Lad thought they were actually
asking a question. So he whispered an answer.

"It's LaundroManiac, but please shut yer trap.
Make that *traps*."

"Whooooooooooooo ... heeeeeeeeeeeeeeeeeee ..."

"Shush! I said it's LaundroManiac!"

"Whoooooooooooooo . . . heeeeeeeeeeeeeeeeee . . ."

"Fer th' t'ird toim," he whispered. "It is Laun—dro—Ma—ni—ac!"

"Whoooooooooooo . . . heeeeeeeeeeeeeeeeee . . ."

Tubesock thought the Two-Headed tyke was trying to be funny, and he didn't find it funny at all.

"Go ahead," he whispered loudly. So loudly, it could hardly be considered a whisper. "I dare ya ta ask me who that is again!"

"Whoooooooooooo . . . heeeeeeeeeeeeeeeeee . . ."

"Okay now," he said, now trembling with anger. "I'll give ya one more break because I'm a reasonable fella and yer nothin' but a couple o' wee babies, but heaven help ya if ya ask me that one more toim."

"Whooooooooooooo . . . heeeeeeeeeeeeeeeeee . . ."

"Arrrrrrrrgggggghhhhhhhh!" said the angry sock as he leaped onto the two-headed baby. They crashed into Mighty and me, and we all crashed through the control booth door and landed in a heap.

CHAPTER 14

WALL OF GOONS

We were surrounded by Laundrogoons in two seconds. They were big. They made a high goony wall. They made goony sounds—like a choir singing in six-part goony harmony. To get an idea of what this sounded like, round up six people—I suggest teachers, since goonyness comes

naturally to them—and ask them to chant the following over and over:

Goink-goink, flubba-flubba, gleebie-gloobie, guff!
Goink-goink, flubba-flubba, gleebie-gloobie, guff!

Some should chant high, some low, but most importantly, they should all try to make it sound like their tongues and lips are made of lint.

The two hugest Laundrogoons stepped apart like double doors and through the opening between them came Lousy Lou the LaundroManiac. I looked up at

that huge, scary head, and it took me a second to realize that the rest of him wasn't really that big. In fact, it was very small. The goons had wheeled him in on a tall stool, and his legs were dangling like a little kid. He was dressed all in white and the white-on-white eyeballs were even freakier up close. He snickered and bubbled again, but a lot louder and with a lot more disgusting bubbles this time.

The goons were still chanting.

Goink-goink, flubba-flubba, gleebie-gloobie, guff.

Goink-goink, flubba-flubba, gleebie-gloobie, guff.

LaundroManiac stared at Mighty Tighty Whitey and Terrifyin' Tubesock Lad. He ran his fingers

through his hair, sending soap flakes flurrying like a minisnowstorm. The flakes mixed with the suds, making more and more suds. What a disgusting freak.

Goink-goink, flubba-flubba, gleebie-gloobie, guff.

"ALL RIGHT ALREADY! STOP THAT GOONY CHANTING! WHAT THE HECK IS A GLEEBIE-GLOOBY ANYWAY? I SUPPOSE I HAVE TO DO *EVERYTHING* AROUND HERE! I EVEN HAVE TO TAKE TIME OUT OF MY DISGUSTINGLY EVIL SCHEDULE TO WRITE A HALFWAY DECENT *CHANT* FOR YOU GOONS?"

It took a while for the flakes and suds from that outburst to clear.

"But first," LaundroManiac said in a more normal voice, well, normal for him, "let's get down to the business at hand. You two—underpants idiot and sock twerp—you would make a fine addition to my current project. Are you interested in a money-making proposition?"

"I don't know about *them* . . ." interrupted Biff.

". . . but we would *love* to make some money!" said Smiff.

"We're gonna need to buy a new diaper," said Biff.

" 'Cause this one's all stretched out," said Smiff.

"I wasn't talking to you double-dopes," LaundroManiac replied. "But, by the way, brilliant costume! Same goes for you, Amazing Techno Dude."

I guess he recognized us.

"You have to wake up pretty early in the morning to pull the underwear over my eyes!" he said. "Or to pull it over *your* eyes and actually *fool* me!"

Then he snickered so hard that filthy bubbles bubbled from his nose, mouth, and ears.

"But come to think of it, ATD, you and your little

muscle-bound double-doofus are wearing costumes, and costumes, are made of fabric! I suppose I could take the time to remove those costumes and let you just walk away, but I've got places to go and people to go crazy on, so I'll just shred you as is."

He snickered and bubbled and explained that after he turned us all into money, he'd *spend* us, and we'd be folded and crumpled and passed among the filthy hands of millions of strangers and be spent over and over and lost forever and never see our friends or families again.

"And you know what I'll *spend* you on?" he continued. "Get this: more trucks! More conveyor belts! More laundromadhouses! All to make more and more *money* and so on and so forth, because money is my friend—and I want lots and lots of friends . . . that I can spend . . . to make more friends . . . that I can also spend! It's endless! I AM ENDLESSLY, DISGUSTINGLY EVIL!!! HA, HA, HA, HA, HA, HA, HA!"

If you looked up *disgustingly evil crazy nutjob* in the dictionary, there'd be a picture of this guy. And it wouldn't be a pretty picture.

LaundroManiac's head was surrounded by an expanding mass of scummy bubbles from all the

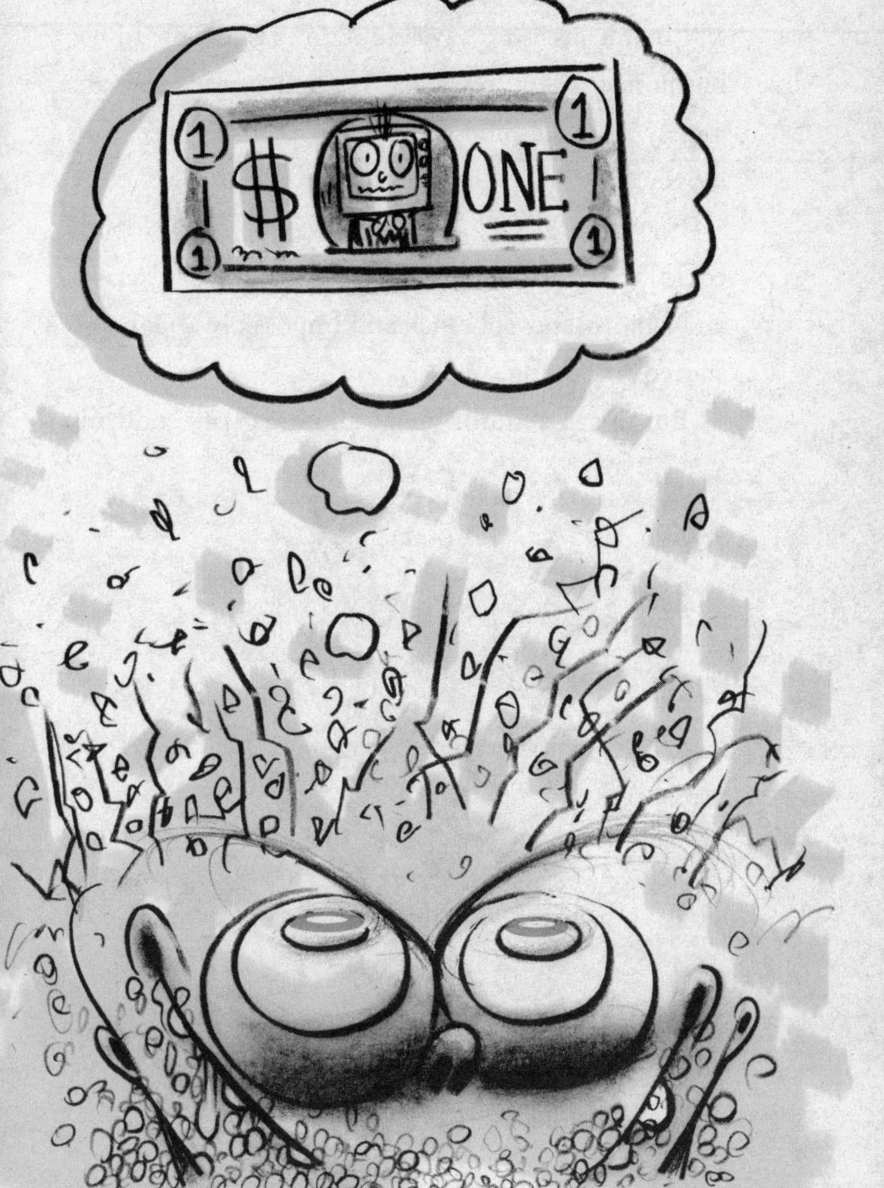
1
$
ONE

snickering, and the Laundrogoons were snickering, and it was just so crazy! He didn't even want to use his money to buy cool stuff? He only wanted to make money to make more *money* . . . to make even *more* money?

It was so stupid, maybe it was a joke! Nobody could be serious about this. So I started snickering, and Mighty and Tubesock and Impossibly Tough also started snickering.

But then LaundroManiac and the goons suddenly

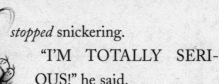

stopped snickering.

"I'M TOTALLY SERI-OUS!" he said.

Then the biggest goon gathered us up in his arms, like a load of laundry. Another goon carried LaundroManiac on his shoulders and down we all went, down the long stairway to the moving conveyor belt. He dumped us out like an oversized laundry load and tied us to the belt with super-heavy-duty-superhero-resistant rope that dug into our arms and legs like only super-heavy-duty-superhero-resistant rope can do.

LaundroManiac snickered, bubbled, and bid us farewell as we moved off on the conveyor belt toward the chomping jaws of the shredder.

CHAPTER 15

Home Alone

Back at the house, the Bodacious Backwards Woman and the rest of the Super Goofballs were talking about how they couldn't stand being left out. They wished they could have gone on the mission. They were superheroes, doggone it, and they wanted to do super stuff, and to be denied the opportunity was like a super jail sentence!

Blunder Mutt was so frustrated, he was banging his face on the floor. He was waiting right near the phone, because he was the official phone answerer.

"I sure that Amazy Techo be calling soonish to asking me to helping him," he said.

But since I wasn't calling, Blunder just kept pounding. His face didn't hurt at all, but he had made a very deep dent in the living room floor.

Just then the doorbell rang, but Blunder thought it was the phone. He jumped up to answer it, tripped on the hole in the floor, then crawled to the phone.

"Hellooo! Helloooo! I knows yer there Amazy Techo Duder! Helloooo!"

In the meantime, Super Vacation Man answered the door: "Greetings! *Zing!* Yo! Hey!"

But there was no one there. He looked around on the porch and in the bushes—even under the welcome mat—but whoever had rung that bell had disappeared.

"Stupid neighborhood kids!" said SVM. "They're always doing that darn ding-dong-ditch!"

"I used to love doing ding-dong-ditch," said SuperSass CuteGirl. "It's such a cute, sassy prank, don't you think? Very amusing."

But Super Vacation Man was not amused. He turned and walked superfast back in through the doorway and then—*bam!*—crashed into something that wasn't there. It was something invisible, like a

force field. SVM bounced off and fell back hard onto his super butt, causing the entire neighborhood to shake.

"What the *bang, boom, ouch!*" yelled SVM. "Who's been leaving invisible stuff around the house?!"

Amazingly, none of this distracted Blunder Mutt from his task. He was still saying "HELLLOOOO!" to me into the phone, but of course I couldn't hear him because I wasn't *on* the phone. I was in the Lost Undergarment District, in the LaundroMadhouse, on a conveyor belt, moving steadily toward my doom.

Blunder finally gave up and started pounding his face into the dent on the floor again.

"This very depressing!" shouted Wonder Boulder. "Ding-dong-ditching, invisible things crashing, dumb dogs pounding dents into floor with faces!"

"Hey! Only one—*pound, pound, pound*—dumb dog demting demts 'round here, duddy!" corrected Blunder.

All the Super Goofballs were pretty out of it.

T-Tex3000 stared straight ahead, his orange tongue flicking in slow motion. No sparks were coming off it, just dinosaur drool.

"I never could have predicted how bad this would get!" squawked Pooky the Paranormal Parakeet.

"SUPER BEINGS NEED TO BE *BEING SUPER!*" howled the

Frankenstein Punster.

"Like, this is definitely not cool," said SuperSass. "What's happening to us?!"

"We're obviously going—*Wha! Who? Wacko-smacko!*—super stir-crazy, that's what!" said Super Vacation Man.

CHAPTER 16
We Gotta Get Outta This Place

They decided that, call or no call, they had to get the heck out of the house and find me and Mighty and the others and help save the day!

"Now right go let's, okay!" said Granny.

"Prepare to—*whoosh, zoom, zippo*—superdepart!" said SVM.

"Rock solid!" said Wonder Boulder.

"There be nuttin' in dis or dat or de udder world what could stop us from leavin' toogedder on dis super-importy missionary!"` said you know who.

Then they all jumped up and raced toward the door and crashed into that darn force field again. They were so spaced out, they had forgotten all about it.

Then, all of a sudden, something appeared in the air, right where they had crashed into the thing that

had seemed like it wasn't there. It was a black nose—kind of a rodentlike nose. It had long whiskers and it was just floating there. And then a furry face filled in around the nose—sharp blue teeth, mysterious eyes, a very hip and happening goatee—then a whole head, neck, shoulders, and so on, all the way down to some extremely cool blue shoes. He had a blue guitar strapped around his neck and his entire outfit was blue.

The Goofballs gasped. It was someone they'd heard about.

CHAPTER 17

The Cool Neighbor

"Hidey ho, neighbors," he said in a supercool whisper. "Pleased to finally connect. I'm your neighbor, the Invisible Superbad Blue-Fanged Ferret."

"Wait a mimmit," said Blunder suspiciously. "If you so imbizzable and so parrot-y, why I seein' you an' why you not all feathery an' beakish?"

"I'm a *ferret*, not a *parrot*," he said. "And I'm only invisible when I *want* to be."

"That is so cool," said SuperSass, "and I know cool. You, sir, are almost as cool as I am."

"Yes, I know," he said. "I'm so cool I don't even say *cool*—I say *coo'*."

"That's coo', too," said SuperSass.

"Coo'," said all the Goofballs.

And they were right. This was one cool ferret. I mean, you could actually feel the cool coming off him—a superchilly, blue, glowing cool.

"I'm way-hungry for our first band practice—it is *so* in the fridge," he whispered.

The Goofballs were confused.

"Question," said Super Vacation Man. "What do you mean, 'it's in the fridge'?"

"I mean it's coo'," he said.

"Oh, right," said the Goofballs. "Cooooooooo'."

"Say," said Super Vacation Man, "you'd make a darn good—*peek-a-boo, look out, gotcha*—crime fighter with that invisibility thing!"

"Nah, music's a lot more coo'. But, holy-moley," said the ferret, "sounds like you're about to agitate the gravel to some sort of superimportant mission, so maybe I should toodle-oo and catch you later?"

"Later? Toodle-who? You gottsa be kindling!"

gasped Blunder Mutt. "Who cares 'bout some stupid ol' super-importy missionary?!"

"Yeah," squealed SuperSass. "Who cares about un-coo' crime fightin' anyhoo? We're startin' a band!!!!"

"Coo'!" cried the rest as they danced around the

room. Every single one of them immediately forgot about me and Mighty and Biff and Smiff and ran as fast as they could down to the basement. All except Blunder Mutt, who bounced happily down the stairs on his head, as usual.

CHAPTER 18

Hot Is Where the Heat Is

That rope was even heavier-duty than I thought. I tried everything to break through it—Amazing Techno Dude Laser, high-speed microcircular saw, my teeth, everything—but nothing worked. It seemed super-rope technology was years ahead of super-rope *cutting* technology. Meanwhile, we were moving along the conveyor belt ever closer to the chomping jaws of the shredder. We passed through the washing room, the rinsing room, and we entered the drying room.

Man, was it hot in there. Sweat poured out of our pores like a thousand little rivers. We quickly ran out of sweat and the drying began. We got really dry, really fast. Mighty blamed Tubesock for this horrible situation, and Tubesock blamed Mighty. They were

bickering more than ever. Things were not going well.

The shredder would be next, and the sound of the chomping jaws was deafening now.

I really hate to ask other people for help, but I decided it was about time to call Granny and the others. Using the built-in phone in my helmet, I dialed the number and it rang. And rang.

"Some official Phone Answerer!" I said. "C'mon, Blunder—pick up the phone! Pick up the stinking phone!

CHAPTER 19

Loud and Louder

None of the Goofballs could hear, because they were down in the basement playing the loudest music ever. The Invisible Superbad Blue-Fanged Ferret was an amazingly loud guitar player. When he played his first chord, every drinking glass in the kitchen-lair exploded. T-Tex3000 made a crazy crackling light show by flicking blue and green

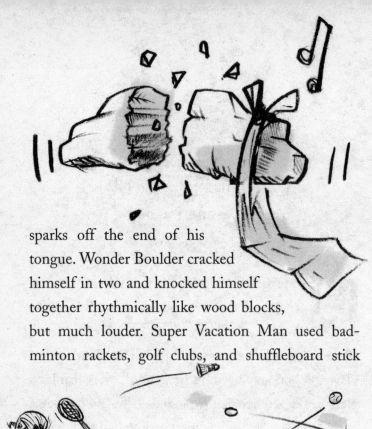

sparks off the end of his
tongue. Wonder Boulder cracked
himself in two and knocked himself
together rhythmically like wood blocks,
but much louder. Super Vacation Man used bad-
minton rackets, golf clubs, and shuffleboard stick

things (and the birdies, balls, and disks that go with
them) to make loud whooshing, whacking, and crashing sounds—plus the added sound of other Goofballs

saying *ouch, ouch, ouch*—all to the beat. Granny was backwards singing, somersaulting, and bouncing off the basement walls. SuperSass was singing a totally different song about how coo' it was to be coo'. Pooky predicted that the Frankenstein Punster would just shake his fists and howl, so she took the liberty of quickly inserting maracas into his clenched fingers, and he made an additional musical contribution without even knowing it.

Blunder thought it was the best music he'd ever heard, and he played the drums proudly with his face.

Scoodlyboot looked lovingly at Blunder. She couldn't believe that he was a talented musician—yet another dimension of Blunder's amazingness. She howled her love to the heavens, attempting harmony, but missing it by a mile.

And the phone kept ringing.

CHAPTER 20
super stretch

I figured they'd all fallen asleep from boredom or something. I let the phone ring while I tried to think of a way out of our horrible situation. The ringing and the sound of the machinery and those two crazy cousins yelling and screaming at each other were giving me a super headache.

I had an idea.

I was tied too tight to do anything, but Mighty Tighty Whitey was too small and flexible to be totally restrained. I told him to try to wriggle an arm free and nail himself to a wall as we passed. He could let himself be stretched for a while and then, just at the right moment, yank and whip backwards, grind the gears, and bring the conveyor belt to a screeching halt. Seemed simple enough.

So, with a flurry of super pounding, Mighty Tighty Whitey nailed himself to the wall—and began stretching beautifully. Brilliant.

CHAPTER 21

THE VERY LOUD SOUND OF MUSIC

The racket coming from the basement was so amazingly loud that, one by one, every single window of every single house on Thirteenth Street shattered. And every single neighbor called the police.

The angry neighbors gathered on the lawn and yelled and screamed, making the racket even worse. Pretty soon, every dog was barking, every baby crying, and every car alarm blaring. The outside noise was as loud as the inside noise.

But the Goofballs didn't have a clue. The sound in the basement made it impossible to hear anything outside the basement. They were happily pounding and strumming and screaming and yelling—pretending to be the biggest rock band in the world.

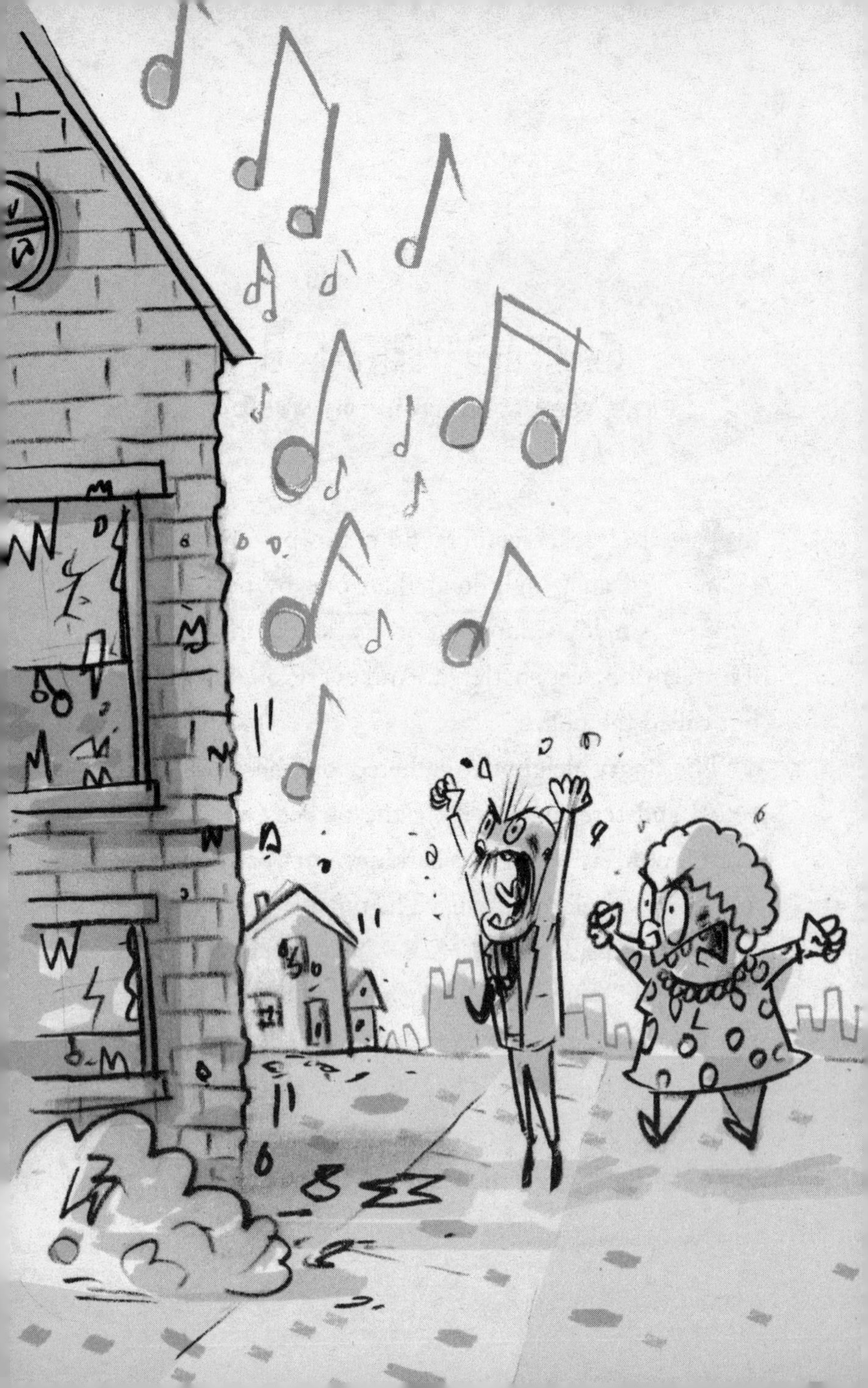

When Sergeant Bub McButt arrived, the house was throbbing and blaring like a gigantic speaker. He made his way through the crowd of angry neighbors and rang the doorbell.

"I know you're in there, backwards lady, TV Head, and other Goofballs I've never met!" He still wouldn't admit that he knew us.

He rang the bell a few more times and then started pounding on the door.

Finally, he'd had enough.

"Stand back," he yelled. "I'm comin' in!"

He backed up a bit, leaned his shoulder forward, and ran as fast as he could at the door. This is the kind of moment when someone behind a door opens that door, and the guy trying to break down that door goes flying, maybe all the way across the room

and out a window on the other side.
Happens to Blunder Mutt all the time. Two
or three times a day. Luckily for Sergeant
Bub McButt, no one on the inside opened
the door, because no one heard him pounding and yelling. So, he successfully knocked
down the door and ran into the living room.
Unluckily, he immediately tripped on the
hole that Blunder had pounded into the
floor and went flying across the room and
out a window on the other side anyway.

Sergeant Bub Mcbutt screamed, "Ahhhhhhh-hhhhhhhhhhhhhhhhhhhhhhhhhhhhhhhhhhhhhhhhhh-hhhhhhhhhhhhhhhhhhhhhhhhhhhhhhhhhhhhhhhhhhhhh hhhhhhhhhhhhhhhhhhhhhhhhhhhhhhhhhhhhhhhhhhhh-hhhhhhhhhhhhhhhhhhhhhhhhhhhhhhhhhhhhhhhhhhhh-hhhhhhhhhhhhhhhhhhhhhhhhhhhhhhhhhhhhhhhhhhhhh hhhhhhhhhhhhhhhhhhhhhhhhhhhhhhhhhhhhhhhhhhhh-hhhhhhhhhhhhhhhhhhhhhhhhhh!"

This broke the recently set world record for time passed during a single syllable. But nobody heard him.

Then he crawled out of the prickly bush he'd landed in, said lots and lots of bad words that luckily nobody heard either, and climbed back in through the window.

McButt didn't know it, but knocking down the door tripped a super-high-frequency alarm. This was something else that nobody could hear, nobody except Blunder Mutt and Scoodlyboot, who could hear it because of their sensitive-to-high-frequency canine ears. In fact, for them, it cut right through all that other noise in the basement and was by far the loudest thing they heard. And you know how the piercing sound of an alarm can make you panic?

Blunder leaped into the air screaming, "Security

breechity! Intro-duder! Intro-duder!" and landed inside his bass drum.

Scoodlyboot also screamed and also jumped into the drum.

Which rolled across the floor.

And ran over T-Tex3000.

Tex jumped up and zapped the drum angrily with his electronic bullwhip, causing it to spin wildly in the middle of the basement floor.

Everyone else just kept playing and singing, think-ing this addition to the act was coo'.

Meanwhile, McButt was running all over the house, trying to find where all the noise was coming from. "I know you're in here somewhere, whoever you are, you unknown loud people!"

CHAPTER 22

stretcher needs a stretcher

We were still moving along toward those horrible chomping jaws, but Mighty wasn't stretching anymore. The poor guy was falling apart. I mean he was *really* falling

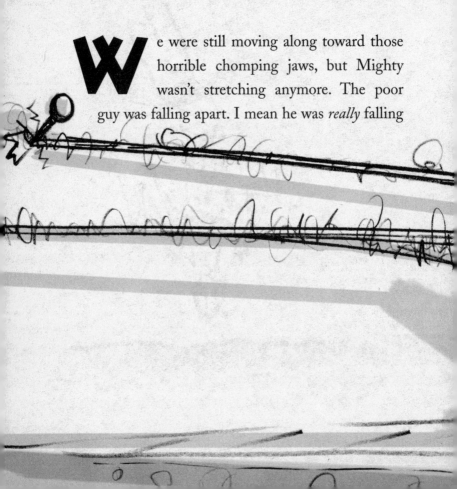

apart. The drying room had dried him out so much he'd lost his stretchability. His fabric—in other words, his *body*—was coming apart at the seams!

Mighty Tighty Whitey had sure been through a lot. First, his parents had gotten clothesnapped, then a nail ripped a hole in his face, then he started feeling like he wasn't super enough to be a superhero, and now he was literally unraveling.

"Without my stretchability, not ta mention me *body*, I'm nothing!"

Tubesock finally felt sorry for his cousin. "I truly don't like ye much," he said, "but sure as Galway's green, you're me cousin and I love ya!"

Then *he* wriggled out of his ropes just enough to grab Mighty's hammer and nails and he *also* nailed himself to the wall.

But Tubesock was one hundred percent cotton, no elastic whatsoever. He started unraveling even faster than Mighty.

The chomping jaws of the shredder kept pounding, and my phone kept ringing and ringing. Where the heck were the Super Goofballs?

CHAPTER 23
Making Contact

Blunder Mutt finally staggered out of the drum and ran toward the stairs, but he was so dizzy from spinning, he ran right into Super Vacation Man, who fell over backwards and knocked over the amplifier, which exploded.

The music stopped.

All the other Goofballs started screaming at Blunder, who crawled up the stairs on his hands and knees, with Scoodlyboot close behind.

"Gotsa foil the intro-duder!" he cried. "Gotsa—me just gotsa!"

Now that it was a little quieter—the neighbors and their babies were still screaming, but they were getting pretty hoarse—Bub McButt heard the phone ringing. He picked it up: "House of Super Goofballs,

I guess, even though I never met them and therefore don't know who they are. Sergeant Bub McButt speaking!"

McButt was just about the last person on earth I expected to answer the phone.

"McButt?" I said, "What the heck are you doing at my house?"

But before McButt could answer, Blunder leaped through the basement door and tackled him. Scoodlyboot piled on.

"Nummers one," said Blunder, "*I* not *you*, Blubber McPeanutButter, is the Fishy Phone Answer-er! Nummers two: *You* not *I* is the intro-duder! And nummers seven: *SCOODLY*, STOP KISSING ME!"

McButt got up off the floor just in time for the other Goofballs to reach the top of the stairs and knock him down again.

Luckily, despite the commotion, they heard me on the speakerphone: "Super Goofballs! Get over to the LaundroMadhouse! Get over here before this maniac makes us into money!"

Unfortunately, none of them heard it right. When a hundred neighbors and their babies are screaming, it doesn't really matter that much if they're hoarse, it's still pretty loud. What they heard was: *"Super Goofballs! Get over here! Your zany act will make us money!"*

Wow, they all thought, *our band has only been rehearsing for twenty minutes and we've already got a paying gig!* So, Goofballs, Granny, and Ferret all piled into the Backwardsmobile with their instruments and headed off.

I was able to send driving directions to the Backwardsmobile via

the satellite radio communicator in my TV Helmet before it started to short out from all the sweat and extreme heat. In fact, I quickly programmed the car to automatically drive into the Lost Undergarment District and right to the front door of the Laundro-Madhouse just in the nick of time before the communicator went dead. At least the Goofballs were going to the right place, even though they had the completely wrong idea about why they were going there.

CHAPTER 24
Dry, Drier, Driest

Mighty and Tubesock were dried to a crisp and almost totally unraveled. They were both just a couple of bulging eyeballs, legs, arms, and two very, very long strands of thread that disappeared into the distance. Mighty only had half a mouth—barely enough left to talk.

"Things . . . are not looking . . . mighty good," whispered Mighty Tighty Whitey.

"You've said a mouthful there, cousin," replied Terrifyin' Tubesock Lad. "Or at least 'alf a mouthful."

I wasn't unraveling or anything, but the heaters in that drying room had dehydrated me, too. We were as dry as the Sahara Desert. The Impossibly Tough Two-Headed Infant was uncomfortable and acting like, well, a baby. I mean, two babies.

"Thirsty! Gimme milk bottle!" cried Biff.

"No, *juice!*" wailed Smiff. "Apple juice in a sippy cup! And make it one with a cute cartoon character on it!"

Mighty couldn't believe what he was hearing. "How can ya cry and wail about bottles and sippy cups and cahtoon characters at a time like this?" he asked. Unfortunately, as he said that, he threw his hands up in disgust, which pulled on the long thread that was once his body, which made him unravel even more. Most of his mouth was gone. Now he could barely get any words out:

"By now . . . me mum and dad . . . are quite likely shredded . . . ta . . . shreds."

CHAPTER 25

TO THE RESCUE

Suddenly, the Goofballs burst in.

"Helloooooo Gritty City!!!" they all shouted.

Except Granny, who yelled, "City Gritty hel-looooooo!"

And Blunder, who said, "Hollowwwww Grilly Silly!"

Then Granny counted: "Four, three, two, one!"

They all started screaming and playing their musical instruments with huge smiles on their faces. They thought they were performing for a big fancy party and they were all really, really excited about it. They had no clue what was really going on.

From his control booth high above the floor, LaundroManiac looked through his telescope and snickered. And snickered and snickered and snickered. He had expected the Super Goofballs to arrive and he was ready for them.

He picked up a large megaphone. It was almost as big as he was. He flipped it on and added an echo effect because he thought it sounded scary.

"Greetings-greetings-greetings, Goofballs-goofballs-goofballs!" Every syllable caused scummy bubbles to bubble from the megaphone. "I have dreamed of this day for a long-long-long-long time-time-time-time-time-time-time-time-time-time-time-time.

"Aren't-aren't-aren't-I-I-I-disgustingly evil-evil-evil-evil-evil-evil-evil-evil?"

Yes, he was. And he was really overdoing the whole echo thing.

The Laundrogoons were lined up, ready to attack. Each

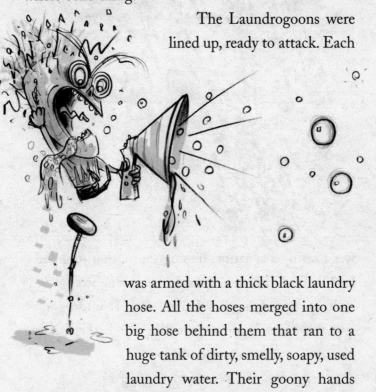

was armed with a thick black laundry hose. All the hoses merged into one big hose behind them that ran to a huge tank of dirty, smelly, soapy, used laundry water. Their goony hands were on the nozzles, ready to let 'em blast. You could tell the water pressure was incredibly strong because the hoses were bulging, ready to burst. Dirty bubbles were oozing and bubbling around the nozzles. This

was causing a spurting, hissing sound that sounded a lot like LaundroManiac's snickering laughter.

Together, LaundroManiac, the Laundrogoons, and the hoses made a deafening snickering-hissing sound that was really very creepy.

LaundroManiac screamed, "Let 'er rip!"

"No!" said Blunder Mutt, pounding his face into the snare drum on each syllable. "You do-do-heads not un-der-stam-ming! We's here to trill yous wiff myoo-shi-cal ex-per-teeds!"

"Right, Ferret?" said Wonder Boulder.

"Ferret, there you are?" said Granny.

"Yoooo-hoooo, Unfishable Parrrrrrrrrrrrrrot!" called Blunder.

But the ferret didn't answer, because the ferret wasn't there.

"I guess he's coo' in a band," said SuperSass. "But not so coo' in an emergency."

"Very *un*coo'," said the others.

Gallons of dirty, soapy water hit the Goofballs like a tidal wave.

CHAPTER 26
The Goofballs Hit Back

he battle was on, but since the Goofballs had
come to play music, they insisted on playing.
Somehow their style of playing was not that
different from their style of fighting.

SuperSass CuteGirl skipped Super Pout and moved
directly into a musical version of Super Tantrum, which
apparently was a combination of punk rock, martial
arts, and a tornado. It was very effective. I saw at least
one goon plastered against the wall by the force of her
singing and another holding his ears and

crying like a baby on an airplane.

Wonder Boulder used a superpower that we'd heard about but never seen in action. He broke himself up into a tiny army through something called Hyper-Gravelization, and all those tiny versions of him shot around the room in perfect rhythm to the music. He aimed himself at the Laundrogoons' feet and made them dance.

CHAPTER 27

A Very Short Chapter

We were still on our own there on the conveyor belt, being conveyed steadily toward our doom. We were as dry as dry cereal before you put the milk on it.

But the arrival of the Goofballs gave us a small dose of hope, and hope is a great provider of strength.

"This is good," I whispered in a dry, raspy voice. "Now we'll have enough strength to think up an idea that'll save us from certain death and destruction."

"Yes!" cried Mighty, Tubesock, and the twins.

"Any ideas?" I said.

"No!" they replied.

CHAPTER 28
A TURN FOR THE WORSE

Meanwhile, the battle raged on, but now the Goofballs weren't doing so well. Despite their early success, it turned out that LaundroManiac had just been letting them win.

That's the thing. There are plenty of wackos out there dreaming up wacko schemes and just sitting around thinking "What if . . ." while snickering madly to themselves. Wackos like that are a dime a dozen. But really *good* wackos, and by that I mean really *bad* supervillains, are not only crazy enough to cook up wacko schemes but also clever enough to pull them off.

Unfortunately, Lousy Lou the LaundroManiac was that kind of wacko. He was just luring the Super Goofballs, one by one, closer and closer to the traps he had set for them. He had done his research. He knew everything about every one of them. He knew their desires and he knew their weaknesses.

LaundroManiac knew Super Vacation Man was a sucker for relaxation. SVM came along, bravely battling bunches of Laundrogoons, when he saw it: the most beautiful chaise lounge in the world. It was surrounded by a heavenly glow. SVM finds it almost physically impossible to pass a *regular* old chaise without lying down immediately. But this one had supersoft cushions (one hundred percent angel down) with hundreds of massaging fingertips, six little electric fans aimed at strategic parts of the lounger's body, and a cup holder with a large tropical juice drink in a huge pineapple-shaped cup, with seven straws and eight umbrellas. Holograms of little Hawaiian girls hovered around it playing super-relaxing tropical music on golden ukuleles. Just *looking* at that chair gave SVM a soothing jolt of irresistible relaxation.

"Oooh—I felt that," said SVM. "It certainly couldn't hurt to relax a teeny, tiny—*oooh, ahhh, zzzzzz*—bit more."

But it turned out it *could* hurt. A lot.

He leaned back with a big "oooooooooh" and the

chaise snapped shut on him like a giant, industrial-strength mousetrap. The Laundrogoons quickly dragged him away.

The Frankenstein Punster was happily pummeling goons with puns when he spotted a large bookshelf. On that bookshelf were tons of books—big, beautiful books, the kind with fancy paper and beautiful illustrations—all with titles like *Jokes and Riddles for the*

Monster Who Thinks He's Heard Them All and *Europe On Five Puns a Day*, stuff like that. This wouldn't faze a normal person, but it was totally irresistible to our favorite pun-addicted friend.

He didn't know what hit him when he reached for a book entitled simply *Knock, Knock*. What *did* hit him were tons of books crashing on his head. Well, that's not quite true. They were concrete blocks painted to *look* like books.

Meanwhile, Wonder Boulder was getting suckered into a game of Rock, Paper, Scissors. He

saw a huge pair of scissors hurtling toward him and knew he could handle it because rock smashes scissors, but it turned out that the pair of scissors was *made out of paper!* Paper covers rock! Nooooo! So clever! So evil!

Then he remembered that that stupid game never makes sense.

"How can ordinary paper covering rock . . . *bother rock*? Especially *super* rock?"

But he soon found out that this was no ordinary paper.

"You know," he said to himself, "I always wonder how me—just a big chunk o' granite—able to see, talk, breathe, and fly. Well, me still no know, but me do know me can't do those things when covered by LaundroManiac's Atomic Triple-Ply, Super-Adhesive Rock-Restraining Paper."

He fell to the floor with a clunk.

Next, LaundroManiac sent out thought vibrations concerning his location, which Pooky picked up with ease. Unfortunately, the information was intention-ally inaccurate, so when Pooky thought she was sneaking up on him, she was actually sneaking into a titanium-reinforced birdcage. Just before the door clanked shut behind her, she predicted it would, but it was already too late.

LaundroManiac set an elaborate trap for Blunder Mutt, but Blunder set him-self on fire and ran into a wall on his own, making capturing him a lot easier. Scoodlyboot went along with him gladly.

So that was how it went. One by one, the Goofballs were captured.

SuperSass: Exploding Fashion Show.

T-Tex 3000: Half-Price Space-Cowboy-Boot Sale-Avalanche.

Things were definitely not going as planned. At least not for the good guys.

CHAPTER 29
TUNNEL OF LUNACY

Meanwhile, ahead of us on the conveyor belt, shockingly close to the chomping jaws of the shredding room, were Mighty Tighty Whitey's parents, Jumpin' Jack Jockstrap and the Battlin' Bra of Birmingham. They weren't doing a lotta jumpin' or battlin', though. They were really out of it. They were so hot and dehydrated and tired that they were hallucinating. They stared straight ahead at the huge, chomping jaws and thought they were at an amusement park, about to enter the tunnel of love.

They started reminiscing.

"Oh, Jumpin' Jackie Jockie," said the old gal, "I feel loik we're young undies again, back at the Duchess of Devonshire's Gahden of Wondahs and Amusements."

"I know, moy Battlin' Babykins," said the happy

old jockstrap. "Thowse were the days—when we wuz fancy free."

"Ah, yes, me Jolly Ol' Jackie-Jockster," she replied. They sure had a lot of wacky nicknames for each other. "But I'd never trade our family fo' anythin' in the world."

"Quoit roit," Jack said, smiling, "especially that Moity Toity Woity. I couldn't possibly love 'im mo'. Not sure if Itty Bitty Pants 'as got wha' it takes ta be a supahhero, though. . . ."

CHAPTER 30
Another Ridiculously Short Chapter

The way Mighty Tighty Whitey looked at the moment, his father was probably right to worry. Ripped, unraveled, and exhausted, Mighty sat with a look on what was left of his face that said, *That's it . . . I give up . . . it's all over.*

Just then the conveyor belt took a turn, the final turn toward the shredder. Because of that turn, we now had a clear view of the poor undergarments on the belt ahead of us. There, first in line, were Jumpin' Jack Jockstrap and the Battlin' Bra of Birmingham. They were still alive, but dry as dry leaves. Make that dry as toast that's been toasted way too long. Oh, forget it. They were just really, really dry. And they had big, spacey smiles on their faces even though they were only moments away from the shredder.

CHAPTER 31

Mighty Lends a Hand

Mighty Tighty Whitey couldn't believe his eyes. This was impossible. He couldn't let this happen.

"Gotta use me noggin'. Gotta news me yoggin'. Notta gooz me goggin'," he whispered.

He'd already lost part of his brain in the unraveling, but he somehow gathered enough strength to think of something. He looked up into the control booth and saw LaundroManiac. He also saw an On/Off lever.

"Hang on, Mum and Dad," he yelled in a dry, raspy voice. "A little less fantastic, not *at all* elastic, completely *un*-sarcastic, but . . . I'll save you!"

And, with that, Mighty Tighty Whitey did something that I will never forget as long as I live. It was heroic, amazing, and very, very freaky.

With a look on his face of pure determination and complete craziness, he grabbed his left wrist with his right hand and yanked his left arm out of the few remaining bits of knitted arm socket he had left.

With his very last bit of strength, he held that arm up like a spear and heaved it high into the air, up past the towering washing machines and driers, way up to the control booth. I still don't really know how, but that hand made a fist and punched Lousy Lou the LaundroManiac in the nose, knocked him off his stool and out of the booth, and sent him plummeting toward the floor below. Then the hand grabbed on tight to the On/Off lever and yanked it hard into reverse. When the gears of a machine are speeding really fast, you never want to just slam them into reverse—unless you want sparks and fire. Mighty wanted sparks and fire. He

also wanted a loud grinding of gears, an even louder *breaking* of gears, and finally the relatively quiet *melting* of gears. He got what he wanted. The conveyor belt and chomping jaws stopped.

CHAPTER 32
safe at last

O r so we thought. I figured the Goofballs would be there to untie us at any second, but they didn't come. Instead, I found myself looking up into the superclose-up, superdisgusting, snickering, bubbling face of Lousy Lou the LaundroManiac. Yes, he had fallen from the control booth, but not to his doom. He had fallen into a laundry hamper. It was hard to miss—they were all over the place.

Laundro gave the order and a goon in a large crane scooped us all up: Mighty, Mighty's parents, Terrifyin' Tubesock Lad, the Impossibly Tough Two-Headed Infant, and a bunch of other terrified undergarments I didn't know the names of. Before we could even start wondering where he was taking us, we were already there.

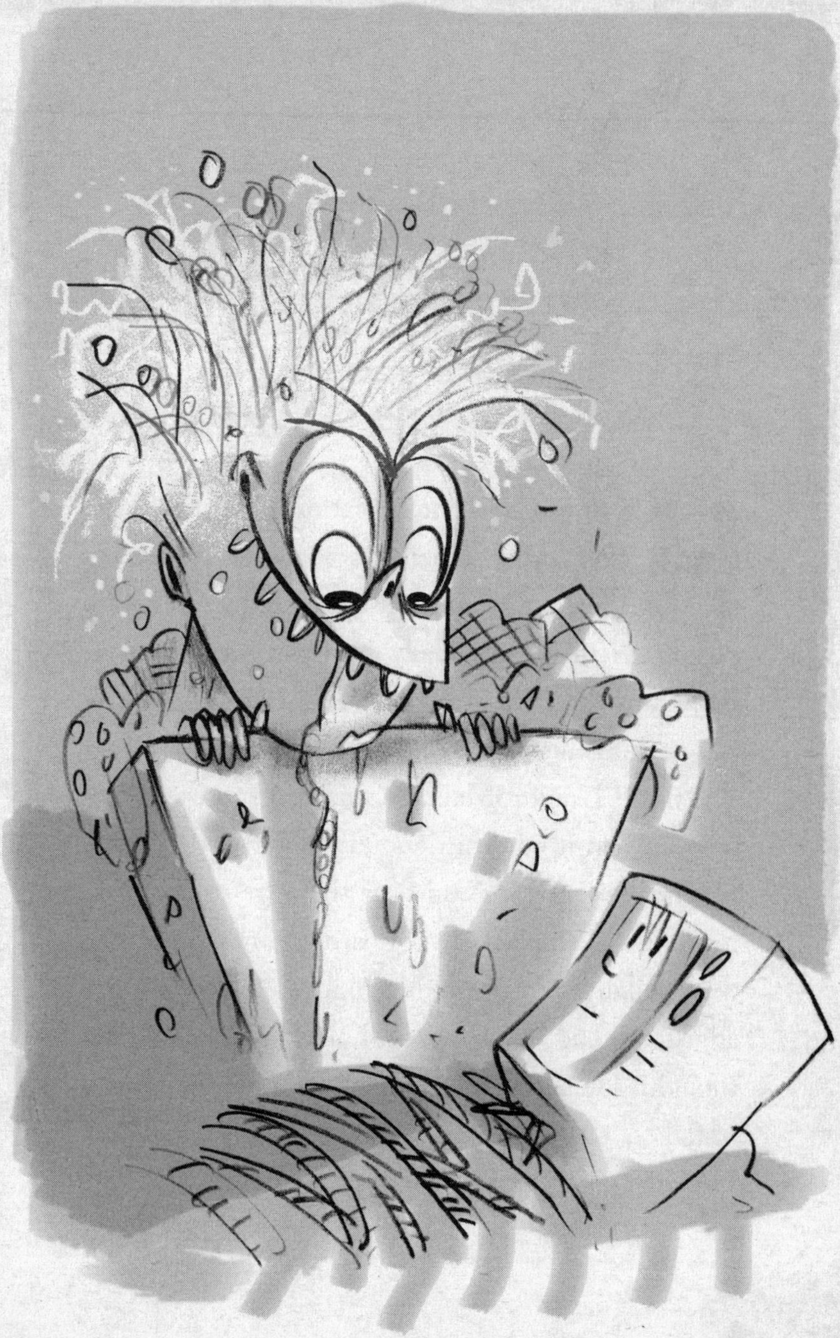

CHAPTER 33
UNHAPPY REUNION

He dropped us onto a platform high above the floor. The other Goofballs were already there. It would have been a nice reunion, except for the really, really horrible circumstances. Behind us there was a high wall. In front of us there was nothing: just air.

I heard LaundroManiac's snicker from way down below. Then it got a little louder and a little louder. His freaky face came up over the edge of the platform. It looked like he was floating in midair. But he was actually sitting on his high stool, which was adjustable and could go a whole lot higher than I thought. He shook his head wildly, creating a flurry of flakes.

"Greetings, Goofballs and assorted underachieving

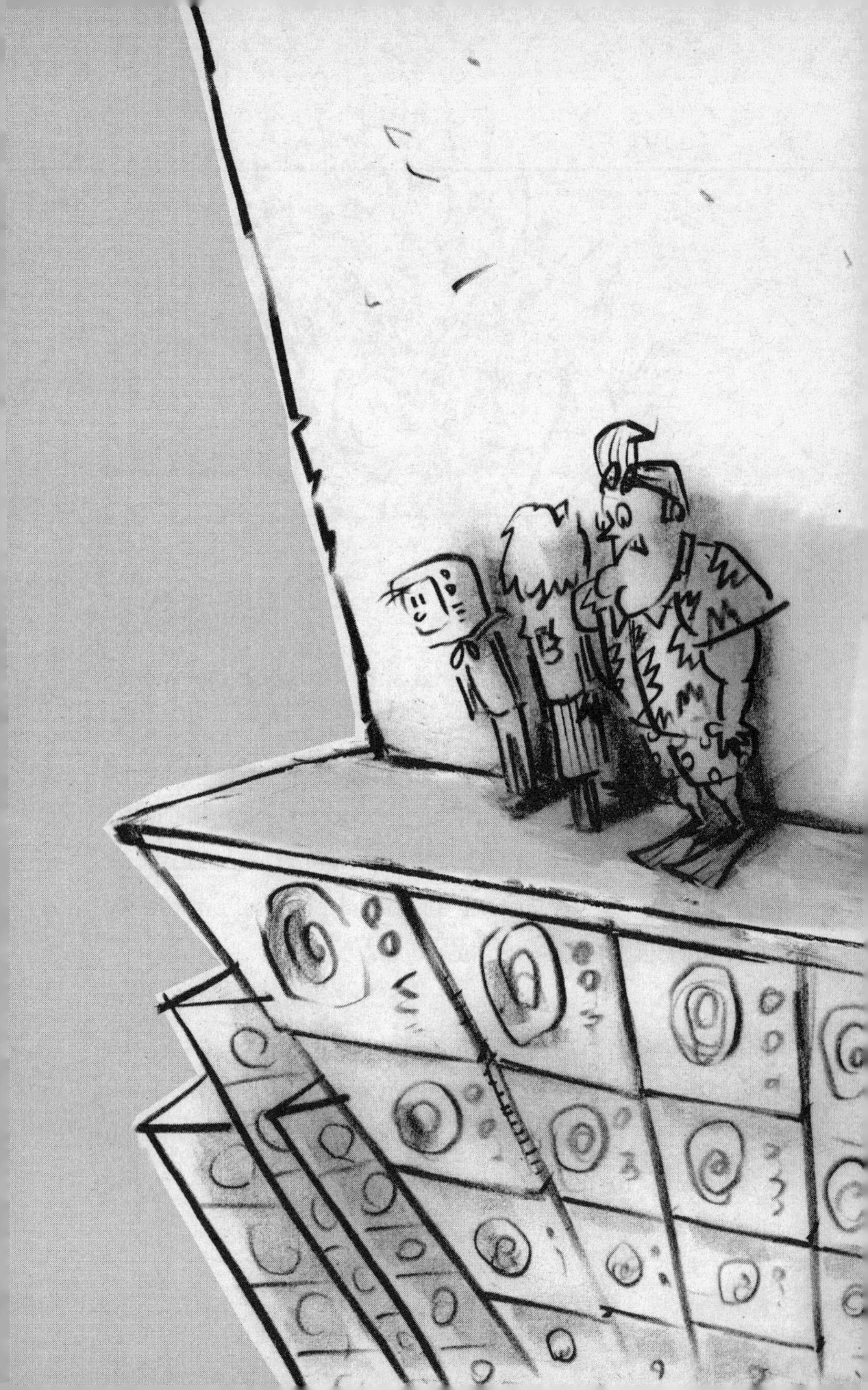

underthings!" he snickered into his bubbling mega-phone.

"Hello, Lousy Lou," I said. "So sorry we destroyed the chomping jaws of your shredding room, because, if I remember correctly, chomping and shredding are necessary steps in your diabolical process. I guess we might as well just go home."

"You know, Amazing Techno Dude, when you Goofballs went and broke my conveyor belt and the chomping jaws of my state-of-the-art shredder, I felt bad. I felt *really* bad. Do you have any idea how much it costs to *build* fancy evil stuff like that? But, you know what? Then I remembered something. When I was a little maniac, I only liked smooth peanut butter."

Okay, why was he talking about peanut butter?

"I wouldn't even *try* the chunky stuff."

"Me like the chunky! Me like the chunky!" said Blunder Mutt.

"Silence!" said LaundroManiac. "Silence when I'm talking about peanut butter! Or *any* kind of butter! Or any kind of *anything*! Where was I? Oh, yeah. Mommy Maniac told me that I shouldn't be afraid to try new things. She said it over and over and over. She hammered it into my head. Day and night! '*Try* it, my little maniac! Just *try* it!' Well, you know what? I never tried it. I'm *so sorry*, Mommy!"

I wondered where this was going.

"But here we are, all these years later, and I can hear Mommy Maniac calling to me again. Well, I can't actually *hear* her. She's far away in the Home for Old Maniacs in Hackensack. Boy, does she love that Maniac Bingo. But I do hear her—you know, in my *head*—saying, '*Try* it, my little maniac! Just *try* it!' So, this one's for you, Mommy. Today Mommy's gonna be proud of her little maniac! Because today he's gonna try something *new*. He's gonna try making *chunky money*! Hit it, Freddie!"

Freddie the Laundrogoon flipped a switch and a

motor started with a roar. There was a loud scraping and screeching and lots of smoke and the wall behind us moved . . . toward us.

I looked over the edge and saw what Lousy Lou the LaundroManiac had in mind. Way down on the floor was a gigantic glass vat of dirty, disgusting, soapy, paper-pulpy, boiling money soup. We were going to be pushed off the edge and into the vat. We were the chunks.

"Laundro, you are one disgustingly evil little maniac," I said.

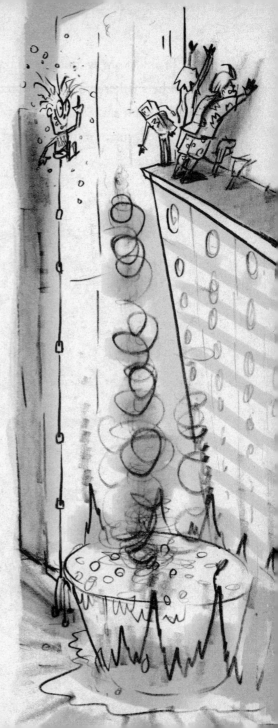

"Thank you very much, Amazing Techno Chunk."
Then he snickered an explosion of bubbles. This time
bubbles even came out of his eyes. They bubbled and
multiplied, surrounding his head like a huge bubbling
storm cloud.

CHAPTER 34
FROM WORSE TO WORST

All the goons snickered, too. But this time they snickered nervously. Even they could tell that this guy had finally flipped his disgustingly evil lid.

I looked around. Everyone was terrified.

I was standing with Granny and all the Goofballs. The more I worked with them, the more I liked them. They were lunatics and everything, but they were true-blue lunatics.

Mighty Tighty Whitey stood with his mother, father, and cousin. And who was that little

guy holding hands with Mighty's mother? Billy Bob Sweetums? I had forgotten all about him. It turned out that Mighty's parents had adopted little Sweetums after Mighty left home.

It looked like Mighty was feeling uneasy, and I was pretty sure he was jealous. He had been the baby of the family for a long time and now

here was a new one. But none of that mattered now, since it would all be over in a matter of moments. The wall was pushing us closer and closer to the edge.

"Well, Amazy," said Blunder Mutt, "here's anudder times you shoulda oughta axed me for help a teeny bit soonisher."

"Sure, Blunder," I said. "Whatever you say."

I wasn't about

to argue with him at this late date.

"But, you knows," he continued, "if I hadder come soonisher, I woulda missed playin music wif that inbizzable parrot."

"You played music with the Invisible Superbad Blue-Fanged Ferret?"

"Yup. He very coo'. He only inbizzible when he wanna be."

"Oh, really," I said.

"Yup again. He so loudish, every window on the blocks breaked. We was gonna hafta pay fer 'em all, but luckishly, we not gonna live that long."

I shot a glance at Pooky and thought an idea her way.

She just winked and thought back that she'd take care of it.

Was there enough time? We stared down at the boiling glop. What a gloppy way to go.

The wall had pushed us to the very edge of the platform. This was it. Good-bye Goofballs.

Everything was quiet.

Then I heard the flip of a switch and a bit of electronic feedback. It echoed in the huge room.

And then—*thwwwaaaaaaaaaaaannnnnngggggggg!*—

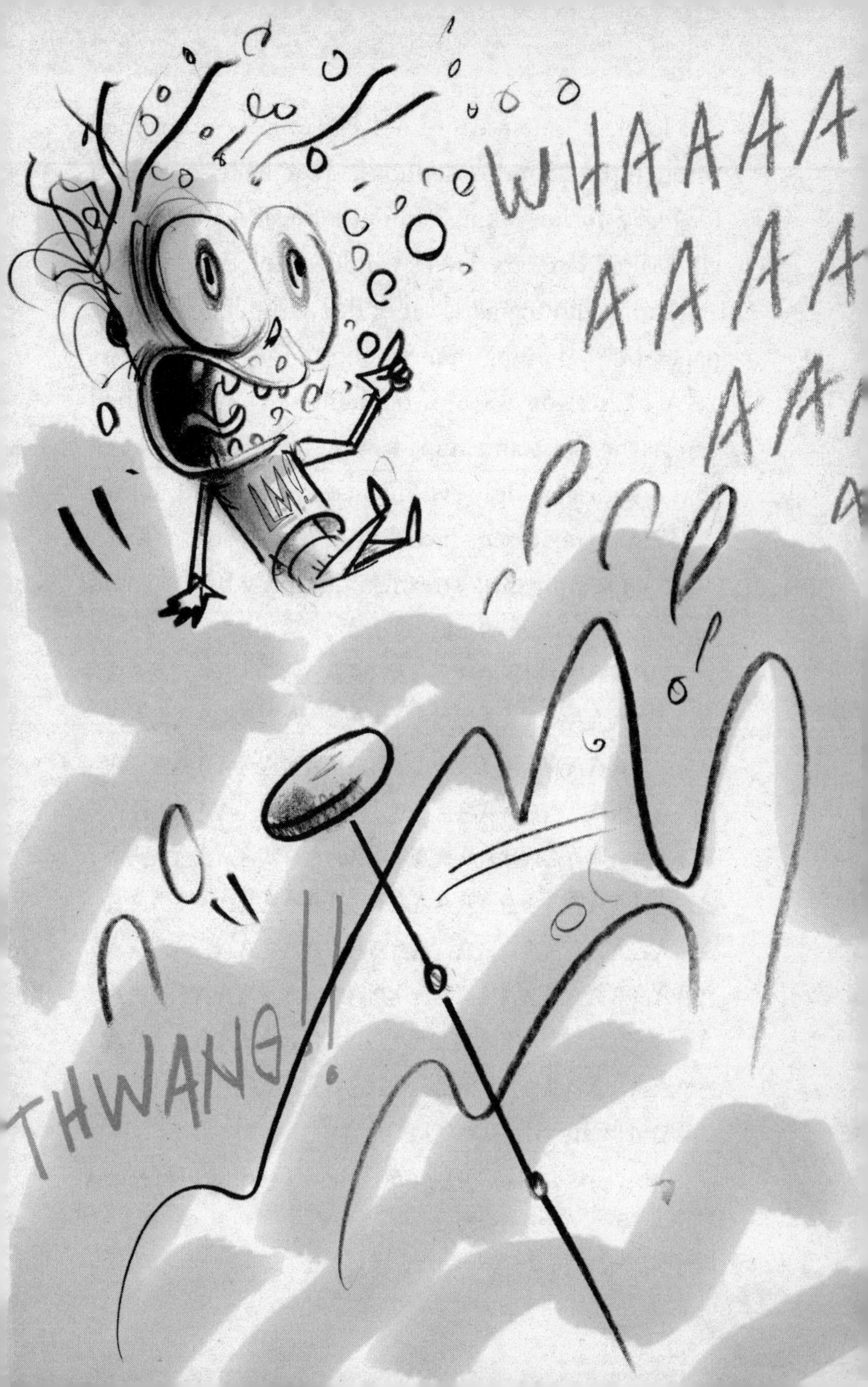
WHAAAAAAAAAAAA
THWANG!!

the loudest guitar chord I have ever heard ripped through the LaundroMadhouse. It actually sounded a lot like a rocket taking off, but a musical rocket. We all covered our ears. Every window exploded.

And so did the glass vat of dirty, disgusting, soapy, paper-pulpy, boiling money soup-glop.

A nauseating wave of bubbling yuckiness gushed across the floor and tipped over the very high stool that one disgustingly evil maniac was perched upon.

That maniac screamed like a little baby maniac, producing a gigantic stream of scummy bubbles and breaking a certain world record:

"WWWWHHAAAAAAAAAAAAAAAAAA
AAAAAAAAAAAAAAAAAAAAAAAAAAAA
AAAAAAAAAAAAAAAAAAAAAAAAAAAA
AAAAAAAAAAAAAAAAAAAAAAAAAAAA
AAAAAAAAAAAAAAAAAAAAAAAAAAAA
AAAAAAAAAAAAAAAAAAAAAAAAAAAA
AAAAAAAAAAAAAAAAAAAAAAAAAAAA
AAAAAAAAAAAAAAAAAAAAAAAAAAAA
AAAAAAAAAAAAAAAAAAAAAAAAAAAA
AAAAAAAAAAAAAAAAAAAAAA!"

And then: SPLOOSH.

"Boy, am I glad *he's* gone," said Freddie. "He was

just so *disgustingly* evil." But LaundroManiac wasn't actually gone. He was merely stuck in a whirlpool of yucky glop.

Freddy flipped the switch, the motor stopped, and the wall stopped moving.

Every goon and goofball cheered.

Except Billy Bob Sweetums.

He *screamed*. Because he fell over the edge.

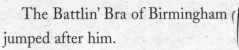

The Battlin' Bra of Birmingham jumped after him.

Jumpin' Jack Jockstrap jumped after *her*.

And out of the corner of my eye, I saw someone *else* jump after *him*.

Terrifyin' Tubesock Lad grabbed that someone's foot and held on for dear life.

I looked over just in time to see Mighty Tighty Whitey falling toward the floor. Ordinarily he would have bungeed back up, but his stretchiness was long gone. He caught his father, mother, and new brother with the one arm he still had and dangled there, cradling them, about a foot above the floor.

I felt a cool breeze.

Then, I saw something right in front of me in midair. It was a black nose—kind of a rodent nose. Pretty soon I saw all of the Invisible Superbad Blue-Fanged Ferret appear.

"You should really consider a second career in superheroing," I said.

"Nah," he whispered. "Music's a lot more coo'."

CHAPTER 35

A Family That Stays Together Stays Together

All the Laundrogoons started chanting, but it was happier, more like singing. A newly named band—Goofballs + Ferret—played their instruments along with them:

Goink-goink, flubba-flubba, gleebie-gloobie, guff!
LaundroManiac not so tough!
Goink-goink, flubba-flubba, gleebie-gloobie, ho!
Off to Gritty City Jail he go!

Goons aren't that great with grammar.

Right on cue, Sergeant Bub McButt arrived and carted LaundroManiac off to jail.

"I don't have a clue who any of you are," said McButt. "But thanks for being here to witness my brilliant hunting down and capture of Lousy Lou the LaundroManiac."

The Battlin' Bra of Birmingham reattached Mighty Tighty Whitey's arm with needle, thread, and motherly love. She also wove him and Tubesock back into their normal selves. Well, normal may be an overstatement. They were both still very, very stretched out. They resolved to join a gym and get back into shape.

Jumpin' Jack Jockstrap smiled proudly and told Mighty to say hello to his new brother, Billy Bob Sweetums. Actually, he said, "Moity, sigh 'ello ta yer new bruvva, Biwwy Bob Swite-ums." But of course, they had already met.

So, it was another victory for the Super Goofballs. Mighty Tighty Whitey rebonded with his family and even he and Terrifyin' Tubesock Lad overcame most of their differences. In fact, although I promised Mighty Tighty Whitey that he'd be my sidekick, he instead formed a superteam with his cousin, whose guts he had hated until a few hours before. Socks and underwear just seem to go together.

Tubesock moved into the House of Super Goofballs. Yet another super mouth to feed.

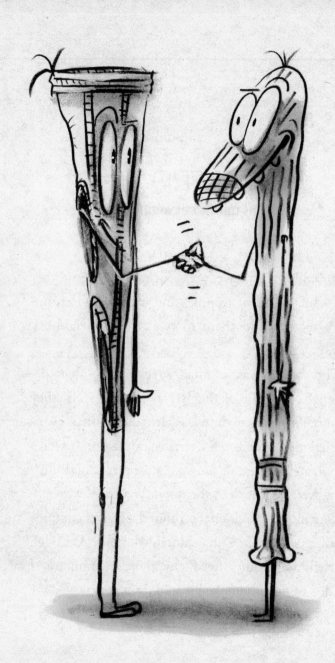

CHAPTER 36

Home Wreckers

I still didn't have a sidekick. We got another huge load of trophies and medals and immediately sold them to pay for the neighbors' broken windows.

The house was a total wreck. Now that the Goofballs thought of themselves as rock stars, they did more messing up and less cleaning up than ever.

That night, there was a terrible rainstorm. It seems like whenever there's a terrible rainstorm at night in a story, there's a knock at the door. And there was.

Outside on the doorstep I found a basket containing three soggy, shivering, adorable kittens. Although we definitely didn't need any more roommates, I decided to take them in. I would train them to be my

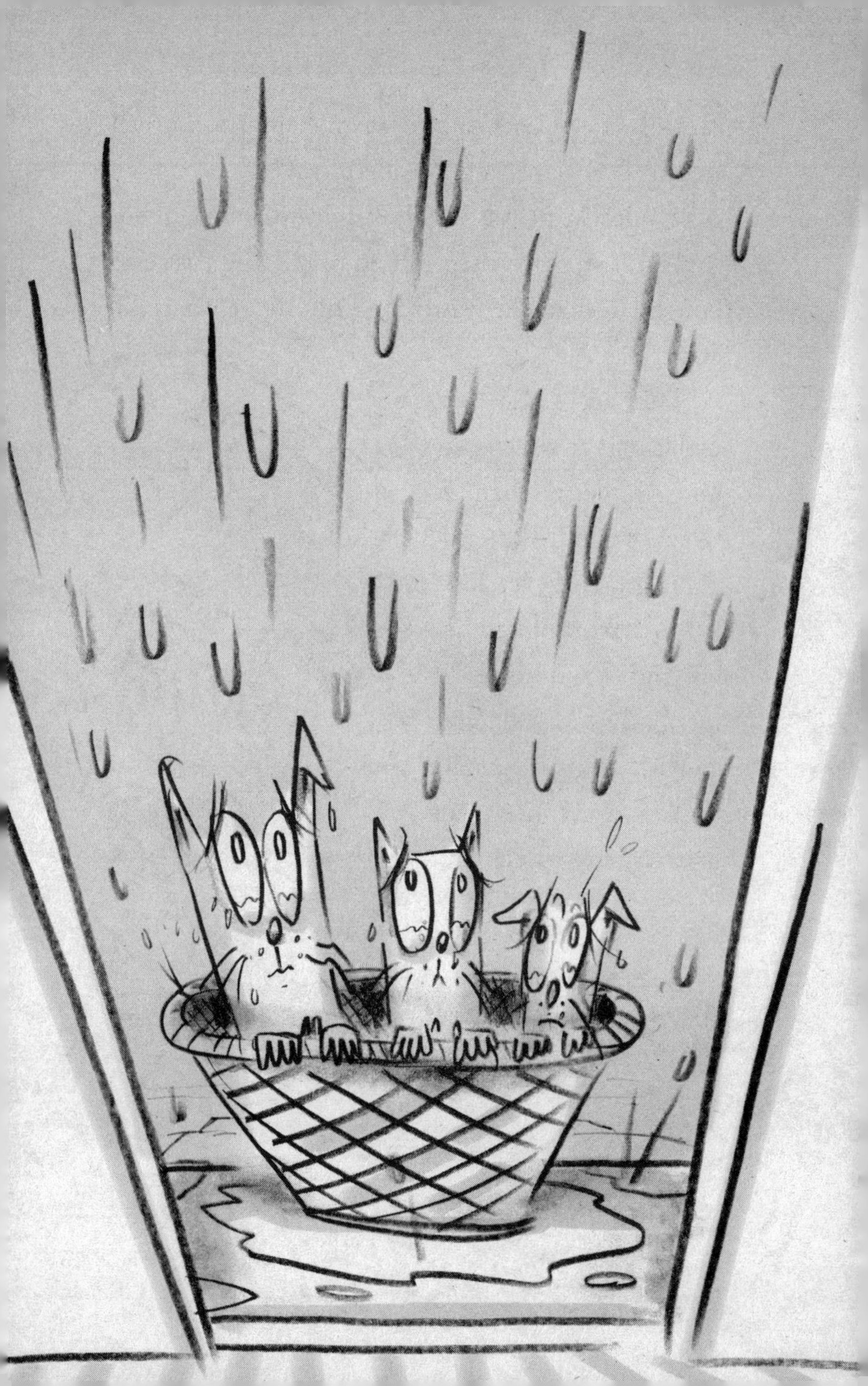

team of sidekicks. I named them Fantastic Furball, Terrific Tabbykins, and Wonderpuss.

Blunder Mutt was highly suspicious of them and would not stop growling. I tried to tell him that even though I realized he wasn't fond of cats, this was different.

"After all," I said, "what on earth could be sweeter and more innocent than a basket of cuddly kittens?"

He growled even louder.

"Grrrrrrr. Somethin's jest not right wid doze little horribull, terrifull, creepy-crawlish creatures. I tellin' yous, me jes' don't trust em. Grrrrrrrrrrrrrrrrrrrrrrrrrrrr."

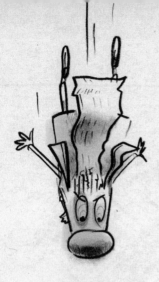

I told Blunder to go straight to bed—in the basement.

He washed his face, brushed his teeth, and fell down the stairs. He landed on his snare drum.

None of the residents of 1313 Thirteenth Street got much sleep that night, but it wasn't the rain pounding on the roof or the kittens' mew, mew, mewing that kept them up. It was Blunder

Mutt growling in the basement and the slow, frustrated drumming of his face upon the snare.

the super-goofy adventures continue in

SUPER GOOFBALLS #4

attack of the 50-foot alien creep-oids!

POUND! Pound!
POUND! Pound!
Pound!
Pound! POUND!
Pound!
Pound!
Pound!
Pound!
Pound!

Sleepless in
Gritty City

There was a whole lotta pounding going on. It was 4:52 A.M. and I hadn't slept a wink all night. Not even half a wink. My head was pounding. Rain was still pounding on the roof. And down in the basement, Blunder Mutt had been growling and pounding on his snare drum with his face, at a rate of thirty beats per minute—for seven hours. That's twelve thousand, six hundred beats. I know, because I counted them. With most people, or dogs, or really anybody else, I'd worry about them hurting themselves, but Blunder seems to have no nerve endings within the general vicinity of his brain.

At around 1:30 A.M., the Super Goofball roommates, also sleepless, had had enough and all started pounding on their floors and walls with their fists while shouting, "Stop that pounding!"

Even though the roommates had proven to be pretty super occasionally, most of the time I doubted Granny's sanity for letting them move into our house in the first place. And their numbers seemed to be growing daily: Blunder Mutt, Super Vacation Man (Blunder's vacation-loving-but-not-taking partner), Scoodlyboot (the most beautiful dog in the world, who loves Blunder Mutt), Mighty Tighty Whitey (super British underpants), the Terrifyin' Tubesock Lad (Mighty's Irish cousin), Wonder Boulder (super-strong, super-solid citizen), Pooky the Paranormal Parakeet ("I knew you were gonna say that!"), SuperSass CuteGirl (her name says it all), the Impossibly Tough Two-Headed Infant (Biff and Smiff: two heads are more complicated than one), the Frankenstein Punster (monstrous super punner), T-Tex3000 (tiny and crazy space-cowboy–dinosaur). Plus, the original residents: Granny (the Bodacious Backwards Woman) and me (Amazing Techno Dude).

The three newest residents—the most adorable little stray cats you've ever seen—had been left on our doorstep in the pouring rain the night before. They had somehow slept through all that pounding. I could see their cute little tails sticking out from under their cute little blanket in their cute little basket. They were the sanest creatures in the house. Their youth and inexperience would make it easy for me to mold them into really good sidekicks. They had positive attitudes, no bad habits, and were extremely eager to learn. I'd been looking for a sidekick ever since I stopped being Granny's.

Above the pounding, I heard some strange, unearthly sounds coming from somewhere out there in the rain. It sounded like a neighbor was watching a science fiction movie on TV. I found out later that the weird sounds were coming from much farther away, from the soggy heart of Gritty City.

Don't miss these laugh-out-loud, snort-soda-through-your-nose, hilarious adventures!

SUPER GOOFBALLS, BOOK 1: THAT STINKING FEELING

Amazing Techno Dude and his grandmother, the Bodacious Backwards Woman, are forced to take on roommates to cover expenses—which is how they end up with a house full of wacky, little-known superheroes. Living with a bunch of super goofballs is challenging enough, but when it's also your job to save the world from crazy, smelly supervillains, what's one kid (with a TV for a head) supposed to do?

SUPER GOOFBALLS, BOOK 2: GOOFBALLS IN PARADISE

Super Vacation Man and his new sidekick, Blunder Mutt, blast off in pursuit of a dastardly do-badder named Mondo Grumpo. When Amazing Techno Dude discovers that this roommate has secretly snuck off for a resort vacation, he realizes it's up to him to track down Mondo Grumpo and save the world (again). Meanwhile, the other roommates squabble over who gets to be his sidekick…and Blunder Mutt blunders into terrible, terrible danger!

HarperTrophy®
An Imprint of HarperCollins*Publishers*

www.harpercollinschildrens.com